About the Author

June Oldham lives in Ilkley, Yorkshire, and spends her days writing in an attic from which she can see the moor. Between books she has held writing residences, and she does workshops and readings. As well as her books for teenagers and children, she writes novels for adults, one of which, *Flames* (Virago), was awarded a prize. Her leisure interests are theatre, film, walking, conversation and listening.

June Oldham writes: 'Preparing to write this book, I followed the route the young people would travel and, although I was free from the threats they were to face, there was a path I didn't dare take. You'll guess the one as soon as you reach it, and my cowardly reason.'

June Oldham.

Also published by Hodder Children's books

Earthfasts
Cradlefasts
William Mayne

Hauntings
Susan Price

Waterbound
Jane Stemp

Foundling

June Oldham

**Hodder
Children's
Books**

a division of Hodder Headline plc

Copyright © 1995 June Oldham

First published in Great Britain in 1995
by Hodder Children's Books

The right of June Oldham to be identified as the Author of
the Work has been asserted by her in accordance with the
Copyright, Designs and Patents Act 1988.

10 9 8 7 6 5 4 3 2

A CIP catalogue record for this title is available
from the British Library

ISBN 0-340-63478-2

Typeset by Avon Dataset Ltd, Bidford-on-Avon, B50 4JH

Printed and bound in Great Britain by
Cox & Wyman Ltd, Reading, Berks

Hodder Children's Books
a division of Hodder Headline plc
338 Euston Road
London NW1 3BH

For Vida Finney

The time is the twenty-first century
   when the countryside is almost deserted,
   when people work at computers in living-work units,
   and those without work live on the streets,
   when in the living-work units there is a tax on excess
      children,
   and when the street people are hounded
   by patrols.

Then some seek other places, passing through
   the wide dales
   and over the high fells.

And one late autumn, two fleeing from the towns
   — and fearing pursuit —
   make an unexpected discovery.
   They are joined by two other travellers,
   and the four remain together
   through new perils and threats.

This is their story.
It begins with the smallest of them. Called Ren.

One

'We're almost there; no more snoozing,' a voice said and fingers touched her wrist.

'I'm sorry.'

'Goodness me, there is no need to apologise!'

The woman was pulling at the gears, swinging the great lorry on to the forecourt of an Eats Bar. Above the food dispensers, the lamps were already blazing. They dropped yellow and red patches on the faces of customers as they keyed in their orders, tapped in credit numbers. Pushed away, the light of the late afternoon rested between the furthermost vehicles and offices, its colour deepened by the masterful glare.

'Can you see her?'

Ren leant forward and peered through the windscreen. All the people she could see had a single interest, food, and as soon as the chute disgorged it they walked away hurriedly and ate it in their cabs. There was no one unoccupied with this activity, the sight of which caused Ren to be hungry; there was no one ready to welcome her. 'I don't know what she looks like,' she told the other. She had hoped for a pretty woman in smart clothes with an affectionate large-tongued dog.

Madge nodded towards the clock on the dashboard. 'We're bang on time. Perhaps she has left a message, expects to be a few minutes late. I'll nip across and enquire.' She climbed down from the lorry, strode through the customers and pressed a button beside a notice:

Interface Unit. One face appeared behind the glass; words were exchanged and it disappeared. Then a paper was flourished and Ren's driver examined it, squinting through the louvred grill.

'Greta's been held up,' she reported.

This was disappointing. Ren had not wished to leave home and live with Greta, but now that it was impossible to turn back, she wanted the business to be done with. 'What time will she be here?'

'She couldn't state a time, but it definitely won't be today. She's in some fix. Sends her apologies for the difficulties this'll cause.'

Ren told herself that it was the long journey that made her feel sick.

'Cause difficulties! I'll say! There's no one I can turn you over to.' Madge paused, rapping her knuckles against the steering-wheel. 'I shouldn't have put it like that; it's tough. But you can't stay with me. I've another hundred and fifty miles to do and, before the end, there's the Scottish border. In other words, checks. If I were caught with you, I should be sacked.'

'It was kind of you to bring me.' Ren could not lift her voice above a whisper.

'I'm not looking for thanks,' the woman answered brusquely. 'Why did you leave? I wasn't told.'

'Mother is expecting a baby. It's to be born any time now.' She turned her head, pretending to examine a container wagon that had parked beside them. She had looked forward to seeing the baby.

'And your mother can't pay the tax on excess children?'

Ren shook her head. Her mother had explained: 'There isn't room for more in this province and they want to discourage too many squashing into the living-work units, so there's this tax. I'm sorry, Ren. I just can't afford it. Only one of you can stay. And that will have to be the new baby, won't it?'

The woman was saying, 'And I suppose your mother didn't want you sent to an S.C.U.' It was strange how no one ever gave the title in full: Surplus Children Unit.

'She said she didn't like the sound of them, and that I wasn't surplus.' Wanly Ren repeated her mother's brave joke. 'She said she wanted me to be with a family.'

'I agree, and it's lovely – not half so strict – where Greta lives, but her not coming has given me a problem. I can't take you with me and there's nowhere I can book you in; that's too risky. You're an absconder now. Don't look so worried. You aren't the first. What I'm saying is, Ren, while you wait for other arrangements to be made, you'll have to sleep rough.'

Sleep rough. Outside somewhere. Ren could remember being pushed round a park by her mother, but that was years before. It had been fenced off after the rumours that the street people trespassed.

'Shall we say, not so much rough as roughish? At least there's a roof. It's dry and we keep the stores topped up. I hope I can reach it from this road without looping back.' She was pressing buttons on the maps panel, running the frames through, scrutinising myopically, calculating, pacing her fingers up a crimson shaft and along the slim, pale tracks that feathered away from it. 'Further than I thought.' Impatiently she tapped the glass as if to shake the picture into indicating a more acceptable distance.

Manoeuvring out of the forecourt, they rejoined the line of vehicles. There were no small private ones; all were large, clumsy, heavy with freight, and they travelled along a road which was hedged with concrete and bridged occasionally with electronic instructions. By the side of it at unvarying intervals there were filling stations and Eats Bars. This was no surprise to Ren. The uncompromising motorway, the orderly lorries and wagons appeared often on the news screen. They had made her life secure and comfortable.

Therefore, for a time she forgot her predicament and paid no attention to what lay either side of the road: distant hills and a bare, endless moor. Until the woman braked suddenly, turned off the motorway and rattled the lorry down a narrow passage between walls, and Ren noticed that these were not made of brick but of rocks which were balanced, course upon course, without mortar or binding clay. Above them more rocks and boulders grew out of the grass and browning heathers; higher still were strange cliffs rising up, whitey-striped and shelved with loose scree.

'People don't come here so often nowadays to climb these scars.' The woman waved towards the cliff face. 'Just a few in summer.'

It was impossible for Ren to imagine anyone wishing to visit this valley, or managing to live in it. She could see neither habitation nor track. She felt as if she were the first person to come here and, looking away, she fixed her eyes on the dashboard, her body stiff with alarm.

'Here we are,' the woman said.

Ren saw that the lorry had drawn up, its engine switched off. A sheep stared before nibbling again at the grass.

'Do you see that spinney?' The woman pointed to trees at the top of a knoll. 'It's below that.' On the other side of them a stream coursed shallowly round jumbled rocks.

Madge took Ren's haversack and helped her down from the cab. Responding to Ren's cold hand, she encouraged, 'Look, I realise this is all very strange to you, but you'll soon be reconciled to it.' She led the girl through the gate, over moist grass and spongy reeds, trying to make the occasion ordinary with chat: 'I couldn't take that kind of life, glued to a computer all day. I had to be out. Not that there's much going on. Every unit and residential block is protected by security fences and even during the day the streets are practically empty. You never see a bunch of youngsters let loose, kicking a ball.'

'You can watch them on the games screen.'

'I'd rather see the real thing.' Madge's expression went fierce. Angry, she strode ahead and disappeared in a gap between trees.

'That's it,' she announced as Ren joined her.

Ren looked round. She was standing in a crescent formed by high walls of rock. Above her, slim trees wagged at the sky; at her feet the ground humped then sloped abruptly and disappeared under a rock. She saw the wide gash. A grinning hole.

'Come. No beasts make their home here now. You'd have to dig deep to find their bones.' But under the fan of a fern Ren could see feathers, a flat sodden husk. The woman put out her hand.

'I don't like the dark,' Ren told her and edged back to where there was still grass. Dropping through the high leaves, the spots of sun danced.

'There are things I must show you, stores and so forth, before I go.' Madge was impatient now; her reminder was an order for Ren to step forward.

Therefore, obedient, she did so and slithered under the arch of rock. Blackness wrapped round her; it had no texture or shine. Her sense of direction wavered and, inside her shoes, she flexed her toes in order to grip the reliable earth.

'Always wait until your eyes have adjusted to the poorer light, though of course they'll be no good at all if you go in deeper. Just here, where I'm standing – can you see yet? – there are tins of food, drums of water, bedding and so forth. Everything you will need. It's our store for emergencies. There's enough for a couple of weeks, at least. Help yourself. Just rummage around.' She spoke the last sentences comically, like an invitation to enjoy her hospitality after showing her guest round the estate.

But Ren heard only the jingle of words; each one was overlapped by an echo. And her courage left her. She blundered towards the voice. 'Stay with me! Please! I don't want to sleep roughish. I don't want to be by myself. Please stay with me.'

There was a movement. She felt something brush her hands but too fast for her to catch hold of it. 'You know I can't do that, Ren.

This is the best I – we – can do. I'll report that Greta was held up, and someone will come to take you to her place. I might be able to do it myself on my way back. You won't be here long and truly there is nothing, nothing to be afraid of. I will show you, then you'll have no trouble settling in.'

She put a hand on Ren's shoulder and pushed her in front of her, not harshly but not gently either because she was in haste. Bending, she tried to joke: 'You're lucky to be so small. There's no risk that you'll get a bump.' Over her head, the beam of her torch pointed to great blocks; they jutted down, sharp-edged. But these came to an end; the floor of the cave dipped to a stretch of thin mud and there was a litter of pebbles, stones, gritty debris filmed with water. Then the light climbed up walls of rock; they were polished and greasy with damp. 'Funny what water will do, dripping down for uncountable years,' the woman murmured but Ren turned her eyes away. She did not wish to see what the flittering beam discovered, the ugly faces and evil masks staring down at her in this cold, echoing chamber, its roof out of reach of the torch. Somewhere at the end of it was the sound of falling water.

Madge guided her down a short passage and pointed the light through a hole; it filled a smaller chamber and slid up a white spout of foam until its pale ribbon was finally exhausted and it was frayed and lost. 'Isn't that splendid!' the woman crooned.

Ren said nothing. She had never seen anything so frightening. Any moment she expected the fall to swerve from its course, engulf her and carry her away.

'See, nothing at all to be afraid of in here,' the woman repeated. 'Also, there aren't so many patrols as winter approaches, and in any case, they wouldn't come up to this cave. Provided you're careful and keep out of sight, you'll be safe.'

But Ren wanted to run away, run out of this darkness, make a nest in the bracken and hide.

Back in the vestibule of the cave, the woman fidgeted with groundsheet, sleeping-bag, blankets. Her delay in leaving suggested that she was less happy with this arrangement than she claimed. At last, bowing her shoulders, she slid under the stone lintel.

'What shall I do?' It was Ren's only question.

'Do? When I was your age, we used to . . .' She sighed, helpless. 'Can't you just *play*?'

Ren did not remind her that there were no games screens in this place.

She watched Madge stride away, her figure lit briefly by sunshine before the slope took it downwards and it sank out of view. When Madge reached the lorry, she thrust the key into the ignition, snapped on the engine, swung round and hurriedly drove off. She did not pause to feel under the seat for her binoculars and scan the place she was driving away from; she did not slide her sights over the spinney and up the fell's steep face; she did not swing round, train her glasses across the valley and examine the escarpment at the start of the mountain's long stretch.

Even had she done so, it is unlikely that she would have paused at a crag shaded by the boughs of a hazel, found the feet pressed into the soil at the roots and the hunched shape held on to the gradient by the fist of rock. Her lenses would not have been able to sieve through the twigs and leaves and find another pair of searching eyes.

'So there's another one,' the watcher said to himself. 'How many does that make this year?' He counted by the colour of jackets and anoraks. 'There was that bald red, and the spectacled yellow, and the pigtail blue with a green flash. No, that must have been last winter because the leaves were all down by that time and this bush gave barely enough cover. And there was the beard without. He must have been without inside his head, too. All he had on was a T-shirt! In this valley! He was soon off. I wonder how long today's arrival will last.'

Today's arrival was not wondering how long she would last; she was thinking about her mother. As she left, Madge had asked, 'Why are you called Ren?'

She had answered that her mother had once watched a very old programme on the leisure screen. It had been about birds and her mother had fallen in love with them all. But there was one she liked most. 'The man on the screen, a horny-thologist or something, said it was a ren,' her mother had explained, and from then on that was the name she had given her daughter.

Ren remembered her mother's pleasure in the programme and she remembered the morning that the ventilation shutter had broken and her mother had peered through the hole. Excitedly she had called out, 'Look, Ren, birds! Lined up like soldiers on the communication cable.' But when Ren had asked her if they were the kind she was called after, her mother shook her head. 'They aren't shy, are they?' she had answered. 'And besides, these are too big.'

Two

Ren sat by the entrance to the cave. The shadows of the trees had disappeared; the light had gone from the sky. 'Remember you must keep out of sight,' Madge had instructed her. 'If you were seen, you would be in trouble. You know that, don't you? So you must stay under cover.' She had watched Ren pull her sleeping-bag nearer to the cave's entrance and had said, 'There's nothing to be frightened of. I've shown you.' But Ren could not explain that when the torch had been switched on, its beam had cleared no more than a slim passage, and on its fringe the darkness had been stationed, ready and thick.

She could feel it creeping towards her. If she fell asleep, it would spring.

What she must not do was shut her eyes, though she could see nothing either in the space before her or in the deep chamber at her back. She must stay awake. When it grew light again, when the day started, the darkness would slide away and it would be safe to lie in her bag. But the night was spinning; she could no longer sit up and her knees were scraping over the stones and she could not prevent her neck from bending down to her pillow. Then she felt it cold against her cheek.

Lying on her side, her hands clamped over her head, Ren saw again the faces that had hung on the high chamber's walls. They leered down at her, they swung closer; they fixed their wet lips over her knuckles and sucked. Wrestling them off, she shrieked for assistance but no one came to her aid. The night sounds clicked round her; the splash of water in the distant chamber grew into a thunderous spate. Shaking, her clothes soaked with sweat, she felt the breath of the cave blow on her neck and its damp tentacles crawl up her twitching throat. Then the darkness swooped over her, squeezed her lungs empty, smothered her senses, and only in the cracks between nightmares did Ren see that the blackness had thinned and had become a tissue of grey.

Therefore, when her brittle sleep was shivered by the tinkle of shale against rock and by leaves crackling under boots, Ren screamed and tore out of her bag. Dazed, her brain slow with exhaustion, she scrambled from the figure that stood under the cave's arch.

'You can paw at that as long as you like, but you'll never tunnel through. Harder than cement,' a voice said. 'And I wish you'd lay off that whining. I'm only here because I could do with a snack.'

The speaker turned towards the tins and Ren saw a boy. He was bigger than herself but thinner. 'It's soup I'm after. You'll not have supped it all?' he asked anxiously.

She was breathless with the shock of him. Crawling away, she squatted by the cave's opening; she could be out, with a few yards' advantage, if he sprang. Yet he did not appear very threatening; his noise and force were spent in exasperation as he hacked at a tin.

She managed to stammer: 'Has Madge sent you?'

'I've never heard of a Madge.'

'Then how did you know I was here?'

'Saw.'

She thought: Since he has seen us, perhaps others have, too. Do the officials know where I'm hiding? Will I soon be fetched in? Her heart thumped against her ribs. 'I was told it was safe here,' she whispered.

He did not answer. All his attention was given to the can as he drove a line of perforations round the lid.

'You saw me come.'

''Course. And the rest of them. There've been a good few dossed down in this.' The blade of his penknife was broken; it was not long enough to be an effective lever as he tried to split through the spokes of metal between the holes he had made.

'What happened to them?'

'You're a jumpy one! Look now, my insides is rattling like an empty drum,' he told her, as if apologising for his limited sympathy. 'It was only me that spotted them. Some was collected. Them as couldn't wait, they cleared out. Doubtless they were eager to get moving,' he nodded towards the daylight, 'where it's said things are easier than where they came from. Or – and I'd not be surprised – they didn't fancy this place.' He glanced at the darkness behind him and she saw a spasm run down his arm and jerk the fingers round the can. It told her that he, too, felt the cave's invisible menace.

Ren slid closer to him. 'I have to wait to be collected. Madge said.'

'You're not forced to follow her orders. You can do what you like.'

She shook her head. She could not tell this boy, this stranger who seemed little older than herself but who knew so much, that it was not only obedience that kept her there but the simple fact that she had no idea what else to do, where she could go.

'Do you do what you like?' she asked him. He nodded but offered no explanation. 'Where do you live?'

He shrugged. 'Nowhere in particular. I just doss down where it suits. I don't mind a farmhouse, there's plenty empty, or a shed or a barn. Any place out of the wind. I'm fond of a wall.'

His answer intrigued her. This is what the street people did but he was not one of them. He was not enormous with tattoos rippled by muscles, his face ferocious and his mouth full of chipped teeth, like the street people that were shown on the news screen. His was a different sort of wildness and he was hungry and small.

'Where did you sleep last night?'

He waved a hand. 'Up there in the gully. The fern's dry.'

She had had a guardian! Throughout the long night someone had been near her. If she had known that, would she have been able to sleep? Would the waterfall have gone silent? Would the icy wind on her hair have turned into a warm scented breeze? Might she have felt a hand stroke hers, not slimy fingers pimpling her skin? She heard herself ask: 'Will you stay here tonight?'

The boy did not answer the question. He gabbled: 'I'm fetching a few stores. You might say, pinching. Only it's a considerable tramp to the service station and I couldn't last out. Looks like I haven't a choice.' He held up the can; its lid was puckered and slashed.

'I've got a tin-opener. It's not like the one at home but I got it to work yesterday evening.'

The boy nodded and waited.

She did not move to fetch it. 'I haven't used it yet this morning. I didn't get any proper sleep. You see, last night . . .'

The boy interrupted, 'I can do without that opener.'

'Greta should have met me but she didn't come. Madge said she would make another arrangement. She had to leave me here.'

'This soup's on the thick side, but I can suck it out.'

'There's a can of meat balls. If you stay with me, you can have them as well.' Her face was red with shame; her voice was high, shrill with the begging.

'Stop it!' he ordered, loud. 'You shouldn't ask. There's Mrs Gimmer. She walked the drove ways. She has tales to tell.'

'I don't want to hear them.'

'Nor do I. They're daft. They couldn't ever have happened. I said to her: What was so special about these Norsemen you go on about? I've never as much as clapped eyes on one. She said to me, they didn't belong here to start with, they came in ships, tramped about for a bit then settled down and built farms. But it seems one of them didn't. He took a fancy to this cave. But that's centuries ago, isn't it? What's it to me if he was a giant-sized cannibal?'

She put up her hands, muffing her ears. 'I wish you wouldn't go on about it.'

'I'm not going on about it. It was you started it off. And you've got nothing to werrit over. It wasn't young girls Yordas enjoyed the taste of. It was boys.'

In the chamber behind her, the darkness had become heavy, stiff with matted bristles and displaced sluggishly by the draught of an insatiable tongue. The boy had risen and was leaning against the arch. 'And another thing, it's cold in here,' he was saying. 'It gives me the shakes.'

'There's another sleeping-bag.'

'I've already got one.'

She was desperate. She had to grip her hands together otherwise she would have scrambled over to him and held him there with her arms looped round his legs. 'What's the difference between out there in the dark and in here?'

'I'm off now.'

'You said it was daft. You said the story could never have happened. If you don't believe it, why are you scared?' She knew that she should not have said that. It was not fair to accuse someone of a weakness that you possessed yourself. Remorseful, she watched his face pucker.

But he did not leave her. He slid down to the floor at the entrance, his legs straight in front of him. 'I'm not scared.' Taking breath, he repeated more loudly, 'I'm not scared. I've had more to face in my time than some daft stories. I can easy bed down here. But it'll cost you. Before I turn in, I'll have need of that can of meat.'

Ren nodded. If she thanked him, she knew she would cry, but there was another way of showing her gratitude. Rising, she thrust her fingers into a cleft in the rock wall and hooked out the strange pincer-like gadget for opening tins.

'Why you put it in there?'

'My mother always hides ours before going to bed. She says it's the first thing burglars — street people — look for.'

At that, they both laughed.

Once it was agreed, the boy said no more about their bargain and though there was no guarantee that he would keep his part of it, Ren was reassured by the preparations he made.

As soon as he had eaten the soup, grabbingly, chokingly, he began to collect small rocks from the floor of the cave and the larger stones. Then he felt along the sides of her shelter, stopped where the light from its entrance grew dim, and set to work. He did not say why he was doing this but she offered to help.

'If you like. You can fetch from outside.'

'Madge said I was to keep under cover.'

'You can't stay penned in!'

'Don't you have to make sure that patrolmen can't see you?'

'Of course not. I live here, in this dale, and the next, and the next,' he answered, grand. 'I'm not an absconder from the parts you come from.' He saw her face tremble and added quickly, 'Except, when Mrs Gimmer's lined up a job for me I don't fancy, I'll do a spot of absconding myself, double quick. I'll not be a tick, check there's no one around to spot you.'

So it happened that, under the boy's protection, she ventured out.

'There now, you can push your face into the wind.'

She nodded, though this was something she had never wished to do. There were occasions when you had to leave your living-work unit, such as attending hospital, but you did not linger. If you were feeling cramped and wanted a little more space, you simply keyed in your requirement and brought it on to the screen, and you could choose the scale to suit your own size. She had never assembled a landscape like this one. The scenes that she had devised had more trees in them, and short grass that was starry with tiny flowers, not harsh clumps that tripped up your feet; and she had selected skies that were blue and friendly. They had never been like these shelves of clouds massive as continents, which broke into snowy floes to reveal up, up and for ever, oceans of limitless grey.

She had never imagined herself climbing up steps made of thick layers of rock; she had not dreamed of reaching tall trees growing above a cave. Her cheeks had not been pricked by breezes and her eyes stabbed by the wide light. But, feeling secure in the boy's company, she gradually forgot how new it all was and she did not complain if she fell or a lump of stone clattered down and trapped her fingers. Nor was she alarmed when the boy stood by boulders and pointed to a gap between them.

'See? Down there is the second chamber, the one with the waterfall. But Yordas is too big to squeeze in.'

The menace seemed far away, vanquished by the autumn sunlight. Examining the stones they had gathered, she asked, 'Have we got enough?'

'Most likely,' he said, and after lobbing them down to the cave's entrance, he returned to his task.

As the pile of stones grew, but was still unexplained, she commented, 'I suppose it's warmer to sleep under a wall.'

'This lot's no wall! You'll not find me lying down here!' he exclaimed but said nothing more.

Towards the end of the afternoon when the light became sepia and shrank from his pyramid of stones, he announced that he could see to do no more building and fetched in his sleeping-bag. He laid

15

it out, the top just within the cave's entrance, and gathered ling and dead leaves to make a pillow. Then he removed the opener from the crack in the rock and cut round the tin lid.

Watching him sniff at the meat balls and stir the gravy, Ren took off her shoes and slid into her bag. There were things she was planning to ask him when he had eaten. She wanted to know whether he got most of his food by stealing and whether he would stay with her until Madge or someone came.

That last question was in her head ready as soon as she woke. Refreshed by sleep, she imagined herself once again harvesting the giant pebbles. Perhaps the boy hoped to build a barrier across the chamber. She sat up, wondering whether he was yet awake.

It took her several minutes to accept that he had gone. She rushed out of the cave, but there was no sign of him, no pallet of bracken or pillow of ling. It was as if he had never existed. She asked herself: Was he no more than a picture? Did I call him up, bring him on to the leisure screen as I used to key in companions at home?

Dejected, she scuffed her toes in the ground, scratching up pebbles. She selected one: That's today, she said to herself, and this one is yesterday, and this one's the day I came. She dropped the three into her pocket. She would add another each morning, to keep a tally of the waiting days. At any rate, I managed to get through one of them easily, she encouraged herself. It was the best I've programmed for years.

But there was no leisure screen in this place. The boy had not come by its means. So he must have arrived yesterday! She must have helped him gather the stones! And she had proof.

Breathless she rushed into the cave. The heap of stones was still there. Relieved, sobbing, she told herself: The boy did come; he built this.

And there was not only the squat column; there was another

object. It was wedged between two chunks of rock balanced at the very top. In the faint light its rim winked, metallic.

When she had identified what it was, Ren crept away. She knew now why he had built this cairn and she did not touch what he had placed there. He had made sure it would be found by any hand that groped, clawed for prey in the flocculent night. She would not disturb the boy's offering. It had been a bargain between them, that can of red meat.

Three

Ren laid aside the tin of beans she was eating and polished her spoon on the grass. She was tired of cold food. Among the stores there was a contraption which she supposed was designed for cooking; it had a small canister at the bottom and a support for a pan, but she dared not experiment to discover how it worked. She bit into a biscuit and stared at the twigs by her feet, at the brown scaled cones, the droppings of rabbits and the dry skeletons of leaves. Soon there would be more leaves, brighter ones; many were already twisting and skittering down. Then it would be winter.

Tomorrow she must wear her thicker jersey and the warmer trousers. Generally it was only in emergencies that they were used, when for example the heating did not function and the repair took several days, but her mother had packed them.

'I'm putting these in, Ren,' she had said, 'because you'll need them at Greta's; you won't spend all your day indoors.'

'I'd rather stay here.'

'Yes, and I don't want to send you away, but this is the best option. Since I can't pay the tax and I'm not having you go into an S.C.U., we're lucky to have this invitation from Greta. I think you'll be happy there. Things are more like what they used to be here. Greta lives in a proper house, not everybody works at computers and there aren't so many street people.'

'I want to see the baby.'

'You will one day, I promise. And we will exchange messages. I just want you to stay a good girl otherwise Greta will think I haven't brought you up properly, and . . .' There was a tear running down a cheek as her mother rolled up the jersey and trousers, but she had tried to laugh. 'And don't catch cold.'

So, tomorrow she would put on the jersey and warmer trousers. They would be more suitable, too, if the boy came again and they ran about in the spinney. She wished she knew how to invite him back. Before, if she had wanted to see a friend all she had to do was switch on the leisure screen and call one up. Secretly, however, she had found that unsatisfactory and she realised why after spending the day with the boy. With the children on the leisure screen you could only show each other round your living-work units which were identical, and perhaps share a screen game. They did not do what the boy had done, walk in and sit by her, real flesh and blood. All the same, when the boy was not there, one of those friends would be better than no one. In fact, any visitor would make time pass more quickly until help came.

Dusk was creeping upon her, closing the spaces between the trees and bringing the night in its wake. Ren looked at the cave's mouth and shuddered. This morning she had added a fourth pebble to her calendar. Tomorrow morning she would add a fifth. I can't have much longer to wait, she assured herself. Someone, or Madge, will fetch me soon.

However, it seemed too late now for anyone to come. All the same, she would check. She rose, climbed the short path above the cave to the spinney and stood at its edge. The land dipped below her, fattened by twilight, its ridges planed down, its rocks rubbed smooth. Nothing disturbed it. There was no lorry parked on the shelf by the beck; no one stood by the gate. Ren's eyes searched down the valley. Nothing. But gradually, peering, she thought something moved, grew solid, took on a shape. And she was running, tripping, slithering past the cave, sliding down the slope, flinging herself through the gateway and on to the road. She waved, shouted a greeting, and the figure halted.

But it was not the woman who had brought her, and however much Ren squinted, she could not squash this person smaller and reshape her into the boy.

For a moment Ren stayed, uncertain, then panic-stricken, she began to scramble back. But the stranger was calling and there were sounds that could be: 'stop' and 'ask'. Embarrassed by her childish flight and curious, Ren returned to the road and waited for the stranger to come up.

Without preliminaries, she demanded, 'How far's the depot?'

'The depot?'

'Where the freight stops after inspection.'

'I don't know.'

Exasperated, the girl clicked her tongue. 'Here I've been walking all day and the only person I've seen gives me that for an answer! Where're you dug in?'

'Under those trees.'

The girl looked up at them, then back at Ren, then up once more. She seemed to be calculating which was less bearable: Ren or the coming rain. 'I might as well stop off,' she decided.

She was a street person! Ren was sure of that, from her clothes. They were neither neat nor customary but a jumble of colours and textures and design, piled on as if the girl's purpose was to transport her entire wardrobe. Ren could detect the cuffs of a blouse and the welt of a sweatshirt and a collar embroidered with beads; all these protruded at the borders of a hefty jumper. And there were the bottoms of trousers under the hems of skirts, one of these edged with a fringe and another with a stripe of hessian; and a pair of boots of the kind soldiers wore on the story screen; and over all these were an anorak, a body vest and a long plastic cape.

'After you,' the girl said. 'It's your pitch.'

Ren did not notice this respect for her territory. She was thinking that she was out in a lonely place with a street person and was remembering what, all her life, she had been taught: never to talk to any of them and to activate her screamer immediately if one approached. Not once had she done so, of course, since on the occasions she had left the living-work unit, she had been accompanied. But now here she was, alone with one of them, a girl with a sharp voice and taller than herself; and she was almost certainly heavier, too, under the wads of clothes. She was leading this person to her cave. With a burst of courage, Ren stopped and prepared an excuse: Sorry, I can't show you. It's top secret. But the girl was close behind her and it was impossible to stop her.

When they reached the high crescent of rock, the girl demanded, 'So, where's the tent?'

'There isn't one. I sleep in here,' Ren answered, and followed the girl into the cave.

After the pause to adjust their eyes to the light, Ren watched the girl's head go round. She looked at the fissured sides, the blocks of ragged stone, then examined the stack of tins. Ren tried to recall whether Madge had mentioned that other people were allowed to help themselves to the food store, but the girl turned away from the tins and regarded the sleeping-bag screwed into a hump and the clothes scattered about.

'What a slum!' she pronounced. 'You ought to bring in some bracken. It makes decent matting. Not something you'd know about. There'll be proper carpets in your posh residence.'

Ren did not answer and turned her face away. She was distressed by the girl's mockery of a home which was not posh and whose carpets were threadbare.

'What are you doing here, anyway?'

'I'm waiting for someone. She'll collect me any day now. Perhaps tomorrow.'

'Don't you have feet at the bottom of your legs? Or have they been—' the other began but interrupted herself with: 'Hell, I'm gobbing. There's a stench in this place like rotting meat.' Sniffing, she disappeared beyond the strip of weak light. Soon her voice rang out: 'Back here there's a pile of stones and a stinking can on the top.'

'Please leave it,' Ren shouted, but was ignored.

When the girl reappeared with the tin at arm's length and, just like the accounts of street people, slung it away, Ren did not explain that it was not she who was responsible for placing that tin on the cairn of stones. She did not mention the boy. She did not say: 'You have just destroyed his offering to the cave giant that once satisfied his hunger by feasting upon the flesh of young boys.'

Nor did she speak when the visitor drew a chunk of bread from her rucksack and an apple from a pocket and offered Ren a portion. Although her mouth watered, she shook her head. When the girl slid into her sleeping-bag and pulled up the zip, Ren felt no relief. She had longed to have someone beside her in the cave's groping darkness, but this was not the companion she had imagined. This one threatened, like all her kin.

The news screen explained how they did not rent living-work units but settled in derelict houses where the water and electricity had been turned off, or they camped out of doors. They roamed and scavenged and were lawless savages. So from time to time the patrols had to go out and round them up. Her body tense, her palms clammy, Ren felt the probing night slink back and a new menace slide into its place.

It had not withdrawn or permitted her to sleep when a voice whispered, 'Are you awake?' Jerking, her hand protecting her throat, she wanted to cry out: 'Don't kick me! You can have the cave, keep all the stores. I'll go and I won't tell anyone I've seen you. I promise.' But the words would not come.

23

'Stop moaning,' the voice continued. 'It's only me. Come outside.' Then she heard the snoring that came from the other sleeping-bag, saw a deeper darkness shift from the cave opening, and she became aware of the far-away fluorescence of stars. 'Here,' he guided, and she found they were together, crouched by a stump of rock.

'Is that other one still here?' the boy asked.

'How did you know she was with me?'

He hissed, impatient, 'Followed her, of course. Only I kept on the top path. She's a massive walker. A sight better than the feeble muscle you usually see, slouching along. Took me all my time to keep up, what with the rougher going. Where's she making for?'

'The depot.'

'I wouldn't be in her shoes if she's caught.'

This sympathy was surprising. 'Doesn't she scare you?'

'Why?'

'Being a street person, she . . .' Ren began, but there was too much to explain. The boy had obviously never watched the news screen.

'I'm not scared of *her*.' He stressed the last word. 'She wasn't the only one on the move tonight.'

His words peopled the hills with watching eyes. She had disobeyed Madge's orders. This evening, thoughtlessly, she had rushed on to the road. Above her, the stars dimmed. 'Are there patrolmen?'

'No, not them. Others. As a rule I give this place a wide berth night times, only I was following that girl. Something to do. Then you brought her into *his* cave. I waited a bit, but it was coming on dark, so I said to myself: Time to go back. It was then I sensed someone else. I thought at first that it was someone attached to her, with a meeting lined up, but it wasn't anybody like that. It wasn't someone just waiting, hanging about. This one was on the hunt.'

His voice had become tremulous, barely audible.

'But he didn't catch you,' Ren whispered. Like the boy, she could not pronounce the name, Yordas.

'He had my scent.' The boy paused. 'But I gave him the slip. I got on to the peat track, on the top, way above here. It was then I found it. Dumped near the path.'

'What? Dumped?'

'Like some do with dogs they don't want. Somebody must have pushed it up the track the other side of the scar – it's a distance – and it was parked under an alder, by the side of one of the potholes. Drop down there, and it'd be minutes before you hit bottom, and when you did . . . I couldn't leave it, could I, the push-chair thing? Not with *him* prowling. I had to bring it here.'

'A push-chair? What's the use of that?'

'It's what's inside it.' For a moment his tone held a hint of apology. Ren waited.

'A baby.'

She was too astonished to answer. He pulled at what Ren had thought was a stump of rock behind them and there was the creak of a wheel.

'I couldn't just walk away from it, could I? *He*'d have got it. I can't take it back with me, either. He'll catch me, lumbered with this. I couldn't just leave it there, could I?' he repeated. 'It'll be safe with you; *he* has no truck with women. And there's always the chance this one's a girl.'

Infected by his dread, she wanted to cling to him, to make him chant with her: Yordas cannot harm us; it is centuries since he stalked over these hills; he is dead. But the shape she reached for had gone, its passage marked by the lift of leaves that rattled then sank again among the grass tufts. Yet her hand was not empty. It had found the buggy.

She shouted: 'I can't take this!' but the shout was merely a whisper. For the boy had not abandoned it. Up there, on those night-soaked fells, among the bottomless holes, he had been haunted by a terror yet he had not run away. Finding the buggy, he had hoisted it over bracken, along gullies, slowed down by its cumbersome weight.

What *could* she do with it?

What she could not do was clear: she could not tell her mother; she could not report the find to an inspector or anyone in authority; she could not appeal to Madge who had brought her to the cave; she had no screen on which she could bring up the correct procedure with abandoned children, if such instructions existed.

Beside her, the buggy trembled; there was a smack of plastic, a brief whimper, then stillness. Clumsily Ren turned the wheels and looked under the hood. A head, cased in a woollen helmet latched at the chin, lolled against the metal frame; a hand, ungloved, lay twitching slightly on the edge of the waterproof apron.

Another thing she could not do was leave the child alone in the open. She fumbled with springs, catches, straps, studs, a zipper then rugs and at last the body was freed; it hung for a second from her arms' winch before landing against her chest. Gasping at the weight, she peered into the face. Pallid, sickly under the weak starlight, it had no distinguishing feature. The eyes did not open to acknowledge her; the lips did not smile. For a moment Ren's decision wavered then under the wrappings a leg kicked and came to rest against her thigh. Ren turned and, carrying this surprising burden, she picked her way delicately through the drifts of leaves and entered the lightless cave.

Four

'I don't believe it!'

The girl was standing over her. There was a lump inside Ren's sleeping-bag and inexplicable noises shrilling out of her chest.

'I thought you'd got one of those dolls. Where's it been hiding?'

'Somebody left it.' Confused, barely awake, Ren tried to sit up, to disentangle the child.

'Left it?' The girl put her hand on her hips, ready for dispute. 'Like this place is some baby pound?'

Ren would have asked what she meant but the baby had paused in its crying and was looking up at her. It appeared to be fascinated by what it saw. 'I don't know.' The child's lips were working. It was trying to smile. Suddenly light-hearted, Ren suggested, 'The baby thinks it's a holiday hotel.'

Her joke was not appreciated. The girl said she was cracked and the baby changed its mind about smiling. It tensed its body and the yells were resumed.

'How can you stand that racket? Your ears must be clogged.'

The child was screaming, its mouth open, its throat stretched. Incredulous that such a small creature could make such a great noise, Ren expected that at any moment the lungs would explode and the ribcage shatter in her hands. Only on the story screen had she watched anyone attend to a child and it was always pink and placid, not screeching and fiery red. Using the cuff of her jersey, she dried the mucus from its nose but that annoyed it and it shrieked all the more. Shaking, she confessed, 'I don't know what to do.'

The girl clicked her tongue, derisive. 'Who brought it?'

Ren shook her head. The boy was her secret. She did not wish to share him. No one else must know his fear of the cave's murderous ghost. This girl would be scornful of that, and she would batter Ren with questions. In fact her sentences were rarely anything else. She was going on now, demanding to know the time the child had been deposited, the age, sex and appearance of the 'handler', the conditions and rake-off.

At length she paused, temporarily exhausted, and Ren answered, 'I found it outside.'

The other stared. Then she leaned forward, looping her hands round the twisting body and hoisted it out of Ren's grasp. 'You poor waif,' she murmured. 'It'll be hungry,' she told Ren, 'but it'll have to wait. I can't stand this smell.'

Immediately she demanded ferns and dried leaves, laid the child on them, peeled off the layers of trousers, sodden pads, faeces, and cleaned up. She would have improvised napkins from pieces of blanket had they not found some in the push-chair. This had been carefully packed and apart from the clothing and baby foods filling the compartments at the sides and under the seat, there were extra supplies in bags tied to the handle.

'The one who dumped her was hoping she'd be picked up,' the girl said. 'As if, along here, there'd be a rush!'

'I wonder what her name is.'

'We'll call her Found.'

Ren could think of more pretty names but all she managed to contribute was: 'Why?'

'She's not lost, is she? Or missing, believed dead. My grand-father's grandpa was all of those. Found is more cheerful.' It was impossible to argue with that.

'Now I want a tin of baby food opened and be careful not to nick the scoop that'll be inside.'

As soon as this was done, she sat the child in the buggy and stretched out her hand for the tin.

Until that moment Ren had accepted her role of assistant. She had followed orders and watched, awed. For the girl was so skilful, her hands so deft and unhesitating, that not only did she appear totally sure of what she was doing, but the baby seemed to know. She did not struggle; she reduced her screaming to the occasional sob; her colour lost its apoplectic puce. But Ren considered herself capable of feeding her, and holding the tin, she said, 'May I do it?'

The girl frowned. 'Not now.'

'Isn't it my turn?'

'What do you think she is, one of those pets? What's best for *her* is the main thing. She mustn't be upset.'

'I wouldn't upset her.'

'Having another person feed her could upset her. Babies get used to the one that looks after them.'

'She was with me all night.'

'And it's a marvel she wasn't stifled.'

'I don't want to fight over her,' Ren said, dismal.

'Who's fighting?' And somehow the tin was transferred to her hand. 'After she's eaten this, I'll try her with the bottle. It's lucky the stuff you'll find in that flask is still a bit warm.'

Ren did not fetch it. She turned away from the girl and the baby whose mouth had already opened at the approach of the scoop. She did not wish to see any more and she felt her way into the shadows until she reached the boy's cairn.

She wished this girl were a picture on the screen and could be removed by the push of a button. Ren imagined herself doing that. She put the figure of the girl in the mouth of the cave and then, without a moment's compunction, tapped a finger and . . . she had gone. Cheered, she repeated the process, introducing a number of tortures such as cutting her out as she began her breakfast or when halfway through one of her orders. Unfortunately, however, this visitor came without your bidding and you could not dictate when she left. This person was not an image; she had substance. She even snored.

'This one's settled down now,' she called, 'so you can finish your sulking back there. I've news.'

'I'm for off,' she announced when Ren joined her.

'Can't you stay a bit longer?' Despite her resentments, Ren was alarmed at the prospect of having to manage the baby alone.

'No hope.' She was rolling up her sleeping-bag. 'There's trouble. Waiting for me. Down by the road.'

For a second Ren imagined a huge figure, his great boles of legs straddling the valley and an eye as big as a television disc pressed against the entrance of the cave. But this was a real person.

'What is it? A patrolman?' She felt dizzy.

'Yes. Or a scout or one of the vent boys in Security. You don't expect I got close enough to see his number and unit, do you? I'd just climbed up to the spinney, top of here, to have a look round . . . and there he was. Down near the road. Sitting under a wall. I'm clearing out quick.' She strapped her roll of sleeping-bag on to her rucksack.

'You might be caught.'

'I'm leaving so that I'm not! I reckon the lorry driver – the one I hitched a lift from – must have grassed. I was told never to take any of them on trust. Curse him! I should've kept to my legs. But I'm not beaten so easy. There's a border in another hundred miles and I'm going to get over it. I've come so far – past so many dangers – and I'll not be run down in this hole. There's no way out. It's a dead end.' Her voice faltered. 'I'd be penned in like a rat in a funnel.'

Frightened, Ren could only stammer, 'Madge said no one knows there is a cave here.'

The girl snorted. 'She's living in cloud–cuckoo–land. You can't tell me Security isn't wise to it.'

Ren thought she would be sick. She had believed it was safe. It was always kept ready. Others had stayed in it. Trying to reject the girl's reasoning, she argued, 'But if the patrolman knows the cave is here, why doesn't he come up and arrest us?'

'He'll have radioed for a van. He won't move till it comes.'

'I don't know what to do.'

The girl shrugged. 'Depends what answers you've got when Security starts questioning.'

Ren's breath left her. She had not been told to be prepared for questions. What would they be? she asked herself. What would be the right answers? What would happen if the answers were wrong? She thought of her mother and the new baby. Would they get into trouble? Agitated, confused, she wished there was someone who would help her, make it right.

Then her eyes turned to Found. Miserable, she asked the girl, 'What about her?'

The other did not answer.

Ren shivered. 'She would die by herself.'

'She wouldn't be the first.' But the girl's face reddened. Then, recovering, she attacked with: 'Only you'd rather not know about that. You take what's given out on the news screen. They don't mention that folk die on the streets, and not only from hunger and cold. Your lot are safe in your snug little living-work units.' Hearing her own words, the girl paused. 'But you're not stuck in yours, are you? Why's that?'

'My mother couldn't pay the tax on excess children. She's having a baby soon.'

'I guessed as much. Not paying the tax makes you an absconder. On the run. Like me.'

Ren nodded. Hands trembling, she emptied a pocket and stroked the five pebbles.

'If you get above the cave, then behind, there's cover, trees. I'd not linger,' the other advised, dragging her belongings towards the cave's mouth.

'I'm not going. I'm staying with the baby.'

'Don't be stupid! Haven't you heard what I've said?'

Ren wished she could close her ears; the other was talking like an instructor on the lessons screen. 'Yes, I heard.'

'What good will it do?' Infuriated by Ren's obstinacy, she shouted, 'He'll come here and pull you in. And he'll collect her and the buggy. You might as well walk out now and give yourself up.'

'I'm not leaving her.'

'Do you want to be put in an S.C.U.?'

'No.' She tried to pronounce the word firmly but it came out as a gulp. She looked round the vestibule of this place that had been her refuge. The days in it had been endless, and the nights – she could not think about them. Yet there had been better times: the day with the boy, and last night when she carried the baby into her bed. 'No,' she repeated; 'I don't want to be taken into one of those. But I'm not deserting her.'

There was a long silence.

At length the girl said, 'In that case, she'll have to come, too.'

Five

They did not discuss the girl's decision. Ren murmured thanks while the other pretended that taking the baby had been her intention from the start. She introduced herself with: 'I'm Lil. What about you?' which seemed to state they would now have more than a passing acquaintance since they were getting down to business.

The first of that was a quick, gobbling breakfast. Then: 'You pack your kit,' Lil ordered, 'and I'll choose the rations.' But when everything was collected it was clear that there was too much to carry on their backs so they decided to put the heavier items in the buggy and take the baby in a sling. With Ren's nail scissors Lil cut up a blanket, knotted on cord which was among the cave's stores, and made the sling rain-proof with a large plastic bag. They fitted the baby in it and hung it on Lil. One rucksack went on Ren's shoulders; the other and sleeping-bags were strapped on top of the provisions stacked in the buggy seat.

Lil crept out 'to make a recce', reported that the man had not moved, and announced, 'Right. On your marks!'

They had worked so quickly that there had been no time to reflect on what they were doing and, ready to go, Ren hesitated. For a moment this hostile sanctuary was preferable to a journey with a street person and the perils of a region unknown. But outside was a patrolman who would soon search for them, and a baby brought by the boy and now slung from this street person's neck. She was already on the path, her silhouette bulbous with the full sling. Ren gripped the handle of the buggy, for the last time bobbed under the cave's arch and felt the light of the early morning shimmer her skin.

At first it seemed that they would never get the push-chair up the path to the spinney. Packing it, they had not considered its weight. 'We could do with a winch,' Lil said, trying to prevent the buggy from rolling down while Ren heaved. Eventually they simply unloaded it, carried it to the top, ferried the goods up to it and repacked. That done, they then had to hump it round rocks and fallen trees, through leaves and deep grass which fouled the wheels. They were still climbing and for long straining minutes the task seemed beyond their strength but they could not give up. Their thoughts were slanted towards the valley where the patrolman rested.

Finally, when the trees were behind them, they reached a terrace. Looking back, Lil said, 'We should be well out of sight, but you can't be certain. We'll have to go this way, where there's more cover.' So they turned to the right along a track. This must be the old peat road the boy came by, Ren thought. It ran almost level but the buggy tilted in the ruts and frequently had to be lifted out. For that reason, coming to a path which led downwards, they took it and cautiously entered a road.

'Did you walk along here yesterday?' Ren asked.

'Yes, and I was sick of it. Now I'm tramping back! But we'll run into him if we go the other way. There's one thing in this road's favour, though. Any truck he's radioed for can't travel along it. There's patches where it's subsided, washed into the beck.'

However, that was not the road's only hazard. For it rose steeply and, pushing the buggy, Ren worked yard by yard, stiffened thighs and stomach for each upward thrust. She did not observe the beck which ran under the slope of the long distant mountain. She did not look at the thin streams which stitched through the bracken. She was hardly aware of the modest lift of a bridge. At times a wall provided a meagre wind break but she did not glance at it unless fallen stones were spread across her path. Nor did she notice how the land changed when they descended into a valley, for she must pull at the handle of the buggy as it swept downwards and swung round abrupt bends. And she must restrain it without help because Lil could do nothing; if she grasped the handle, the baby was bounced violently in the sling and screamed with fear.

Ren did not know how far they had gone or how many miles lay ahead of them. Her focus was on the buggy, on the pain in her back and neck, and the words in her head were: I must not stop; we have to get away from that man. Until at last she heard Lil say, 'Time for a halt.'

Resting her arms on the handle of the buggy, Ren looked up and saw that the hills round her were green and silken. Shrubs and hawthorn red with berries were rooted among the rubble of walls. She was standing under tall branches that sprouted from a thick wattle hedge.

Lil pointed. 'There's an old barn in that field.'

Using her last energy, Ren stumbled after her. She heard Lil say, 'The roof's down that end but it's dry over here,' and, 'Where's that feed?' She had a memory of helping to search for it, of Found sucking fiercely at the bottle, her fingers gripping Lil's wrist, of Lil saying: 'I reckon we can get our heads down for a bit.' Then she dropped into a corner and felt the scratch of straw.

They did not sleep long. Found's crying woke them. 'She's hungry again,' Lil announced unnecessarily. 'When she's scoffed all the feed in that flask, we'll have to scout for water to make up more.'

'I have to go outside,' Ren told her. It seemed years since she had sat on a proper lavatory. 'Do you suppose it's safe?'

'Well, you're not doing it in *here*. You won't be seen by the wall. Visibility's poor at dusk.'

Probably for that reason and because she was not fully awake, Ren did not see the mound of clothes until she stumbled into it. And it said, 'Careful now. You should wait till you've found your night eyes.'

Ren cried out and would have run back but twig fingers, their roots in matted mittens, latched over her belt.

'Now, now, there's no need for silliness. I was waiting till you had your nap out, but the young one put a stop to that, didn't she?'

'I don't know who you are.'

'You think I'm a witch, don't you? Well, have I a wart on my nose or a pointed hat or a broomstick? Have I got a cat? Here, Puss! Puss!' The old woman cackled. 'Like it says in your story-books.'

Ren dared not tell her that there were no books in the living-work units; they were deemed unnecessary since the tenants were provided with a complete bank of screens. But the story screen had often had pictures of witches on it and to Ren's surprise she discovered that they had missed something out. Although they made a witch stringy and ill-looking, they gave no hint of her smell. This old woman's came from her filthy clothes and gushed on her breath: frowsty, sweaty, rank with the stink of animals and mouldering earth. Ren felt stifled.

'How did you know we were here?'

'I don't have a telephone instrument or one of those picture machines but there isn't much I miss.' She released Ren's belt and folded her arms, complacent. 'I knew there was only the one to start with, a poor chick shovelled out of its nest, and I learnt there was an infant in the party before I heard the noise of its mithering.'

'Who told you?'

'You won't get an answer lest I see fit. It's best to keep counsel. Take my advice on that.'

'Yes,' Ren agreed, wanting to get away from this old woman. 'You'll have to excuse me.'

'By all means; it's natural. But I'd not squat by those nettles. They'll sting your bum.'

This was embarrassing. 'I meant, I ought to be helping Lil.'

To her annoyance, the woman got up. 'It's about time I had a look at this baby,' she said and followed Ren to the entrance of the barn.

Found was sitting in the buggy drumming her heels and watching Lil decant her feed from the flask into the bottle.

'We've got a visitor,' Ren warned her.

Turning, Lil saw the stranger. She stiffened, her head lifted and a hand scrambled under the layers of clothing as if making a search.

'She heard us come.'

'Funny we didn't hear her,' Lil said, keeping her eyes on the woman.

'She would need bat ears to catch a whisper of me,' the woman addressed the baby and the clapper in her throat whirred, satiric. Startled, Found turned her head and examined the stranger.

'What do you want?' Lil demanded.

'Now isn't she the edgy one? But we mustn't blame her. It's the way she's had to live,' the woman confided to Found. 'We know about her kind, don't we? I've met one or two. Prime chaps they were, but I couldn't do with some of their practices. So you tell her that, if it's a knife she's rummaging for, she can save her labour. I'm only here to see how you thrive, and you don't look to be doing so badly, all things considered. Nevertheless, you'll be growing tired of those tins. I've brought you half a pint of the best.'

Opening her coat, she unhooked a can from her belt. A white liquid dribbled over its sides.

'What's that?' Lil intervened.

'Better than anything there is in those carriers.' She creaked down and peered into the child's smooth face. Her own was wrinkled and dry; there was a fringe of hairs round the lips that murmured: 'Your nursemaids aren't happy with this, I can tell, but it's for you to decide. You'll like it; it's got more body than that thin stuff you get given, and it's still warm, straight from the teat.' She unscrewed the lid of the can, poured some of the milk into it and, cupping the small head in her palm, she pushed it against the rim. For a moment the other resisted; she tucked her lips together and drew back, but feeling the splash of liquid, she frowned, extended an adventuring tongue, and licked. Interested, she stretched her neck, made a slit of her mouth and opened her throat to an experimental trickle. 'No matter if it catches your breath,' the other soothed as the child spluttered. 'It's a bit on the strong side for a little one, but you won't taste anything better.'

Found may not have agreed but she was very thirsty. After a gasp and a cough, she locked her gums over the side of the lid and, her feet pounding, her shoulders jerking to the rhythm of snorting gulps, she drank.

'What was that?' Lil asked again, her voice loud. All the time the baby had been taking the drink, she had been trying to prevent it, had tried to make a grab, but the woman had held her off. Now she pounced, heaved, and with the child held tightly against her, she shouted, 'You shouldn't interfere. Keep out of the way! Who are you, anyway? Barging in and pouring stuff down her. And look at her, after she's had it! It must be poisonous. She's going to be sick.'

For the child's expression had become intense; her cheeks swelled and strained.

'Little she knows about infants, but you'll learn her, won't you?' The woman still spoke to Found. 'Only I suppose she'd rather not notice you're filling your breeches. Give her something to do, the ungrateful hussy.' She rose. Dignified but trembling, she continued, 'You just tell her Annie Gimmer doesn't go about serving out poison to little ones, though I might be in two minds about tipping it down the gullets of some people I've met. It's been a pleasure

38

meeting you, my beauty, but I don't think I'll visit again.'

'You aren't invited.'

The woman ignored her. 'To be truthful, I wouldn't have bothered. I've enough to do tending on myself; but I promised to see how you are doing, little one, and I can see you're in vigour. I wish you all the luck the good spirits dole out. You'll need it.'

'Who did you promise?' But Lil received no answer. Annie Gimmer had gone.

'Do you know what the old crone was on about, Ren? Was it you asked her to come here and inspect?'

Ren shook her head and moved to the gap in the barn wall where the door had once hung.

'Why did you bring her?' Lil stressed the last word as if Ren, having met hundreds of people, had made a poor choice.

'She was sitting outside.' Ren was thinking: She called herself Annie Gimmer; the boy mentioned her; he said she had walked the drove ways; I don't know what they are, but she is a friend of the boy.

Annie Gimmer had stopped a little distance from the barn. The slight wind ruffled her garments until, discovering that the thin body offered no resistance, it grew bold and began to snatch.

'You hurt her feelings,' Ren rebuked, and could not believe her daring.

'Some chance of that!'

Watching the old woman, Ren saw her head sag; a sleeve was inched up and was wiped across the face. Then with head down, bent as if she carried a crippling load, she began to walk, slowly, slowly, towards the lane. 'I have to go after her.'

'Don't be a fool. She knows something. She knows this baby was dumped.'

'She only wanted to help.'

'Ren, folks like her are hard-bitten, really tough.'

And how do you describe yourself and the street people? Ren asked silently.

'You've a lot to learn.'

'I know. I keep being told.' Tramps were not to be seen near the living-work units so Ren had no one to compare Annie with. It was difficult to judge for herself. Her body was heavy with weariness; her stomach was a hollow cavern echoing with memories of food; her brain did not seem to be contained in her head but had floated away. She stepped over the cracked threshold. 'I've got to go to her.'

'Ren! Be careful.' Lil's voice was shrill as it followed her. 'She could be in the pay of Security. She'd be useful. Passing on the whereabouts of people she's sighted.'

'You said the milk was poisonous.'

'She stinks.'

'So do we,' Ren called back, her mind clear for a moment. 'I'm surprised you hadn't smelled that!'

Six

Although Annie Gimmer's pace was slow, Ren found it difficult to catch her up. Her legs were stiff and unwieldy; her arms would not swing. Also the emptiness in her stomach did not make her body lighter but more cumbersome. 'I've come to apologise,' she practised and did not know she was repeating the sentence until she heard: 'Have you?' and discovered the other had halted her steps.

'Yes. Lil shouldn't have said that.'

'Are those your words, or hers?' To Ren's silence, she answered, 'I thought so. I would be more forgiving if it was her put herself out.'

'She didn't mean it.'

Annie Gimmer stared until Ren blushed at the lie. Satisfied, she observed, sympathetic, 'I can see you need nourishment. You come along with me.'

'I have to keep hidden. A patrolman might see me.'

'Not he. There's none of their breed travelling this dale on this autumn evening.'

So Ren walked with Annie Gimmer down the narrow lane, and by her side she felt no apprehension. The twilight was deepening but she could see they were passing by cottages and at their windows were no curious eyes. Their panes were encrusted with the pollen and leaves of many seasons and streaked with the dried skeins of rain. Grass whiskered the sills and the doorsteps. At the holes where stone tiles had slipped down, the roof beams were exposed.

'Doesn't anyone live there?' she asked.

'Not permanent. They're handy for travellers and strays, but now and again you'll find a place done up. What they call a holiday residence.'

There was a larger building which Ren supposed must have once been a farm. By the door was a small box-like construction which she knew from cartoons was a kennel for dogs. A chain curled out of it. Near by was a low shed. 'What's that?'

'Cow parlour, as was. That's all done away with. The beasts aren't here any more. With the sort of rearing there is nowadays, they can be kept just as well on the spot, in town factories.'

'Is that why everyone has gone?'

'Mostly. Folk can't live on air.' She laughed. 'Though I have a good try.'

Still pegged to a clothes-line was a child's woollen hat. It was shrunken and matted; the thread in its tassle had been plucked by inquisitive beaks. Looking at it, Ren thought she would cry.

'A few have stayed,' Annie Gimmer was telling her. 'Where they can eke out enough to get by, and you'll still see sheep near the tops, which means shepherds, one or two.'

They had reached a cluster of sheds and the litter of farming tools gnawed by rust. Behind was a stone barn. The old woman led Ren to it. Under what remained of the roof was a manger lined with straw and a metal pot balanced on glowing embers.

'Sit you down,' Annie Gimmer ordered.

It was a delicious meal Ren ate there. Later she was told that the meat was rabbit which Annie Gimmer had snared and that other flavours were from herbs that remained in the untended gardens. The thick unleavened biscuit had been cooked at the edge of the woman's improvised hearth. 'I call it my backstone. I don't choose to use the kitchen,' she said, pointing towards the farm. 'An empty house has echoes, and they're jealous of their rights. I keep to the barns where I can see sky. Lathes were always my lodging, when I was a travelling woman.'

'The boy told me.'

Annie Gimmer nodded, showing no surprise. 'He's not a bad lad. He's shaping, a credit to his nurture though I say it as shouldn't, since it was me brought him up.'

Ren thought: Then why does he call her *Mrs* Gimmer? It was too formal. She asked, 'Where has he gone?'

'Who can say? He'll come if he's hungry. There's no telling when he'll turn up.'

Ren agreed. 'When he brought the baby, he came in the middle of the night!' She added, 'Last night,' surprised because it seemed so far away.

Annie Gimmer nodded. 'The young rapscallion keeps unchristian hours. But it seems what he did was sensible, and I've done as promised: I've had a squint at the babe. There's naught else I can offer. I'm past fostering.' She took Ren's plate and smiled to see it was polished clean. 'Now you've got food inside you, it's time you were off.'

Obedient, she rose. 'I don't know where I should be off to. Someone is after us; Lil says we're being tracked down. And now there is the baby.' Suddenly she was confiding, describing how she came to be in that valley, how the arrangement had gone wrong. She forgot her weariness; she lost her timidity; she was unaware of any effort to talk. The words came nudging, jostling, and then hurtling off her tongue until everything had been said.

'My goodness, what a tale! I must say you were a brave little creature in that cave, sticking it out by yourself.' The wrinkles chequering her face were caressed to delicate shadows by her smile. 'Since you can do that, I'd judge there's not a deal that'll best you.'

Ren blushed at the compliment. 'But now Madge won't know where to look for me.'

'She'll contrive; and just you remember what your mother said. She wasn't telling stories. Where that Greta lives is a nice place for a young one. So my advice is set course for her.'

'I don't know the name of the service station.'

'You can unriddle that in due time. When you're given the hunting one the slip. That's first job. Since you're certain there's a body stalking.' Her eyes left Ren and focused beyond her, among the tumbledown sheds. 'I'll have to do some considering.'

'Will you help us?'

'I'll think on, haven't I said?' Her voice rose, suddenly querulous. 'I'm not so young as I was. I can't be doing with marching over these tops with two young maids on the run and a scrap in arms. But you're a good girl, not above yourself like that other. So you do as you're bid and stay in that lathe till I've worked out what's to be done with you. Now make yourself scarce.'

'Thank you for the stew.' She remembered to be polite although the old woman's hand was over her elbow, pinching her to go. 'I should have kept some. Lil would have enjoyed it.'

In answer, Annie Gimmer scraped out the pot on to a tin plate.

'I didn't say that in order to scrounge some more,' Ren protested.

'Then you should have done. What words I've exchanged with that bossyboots is no matter. She has a sharp tongue on her but she's to be praised, the way she tends on that child.'

Ren nodded. She would have described the thoroughness of Lil's care but the hand on her elbow had begun to push and she was being steered out of the barn.

On the lane, Ren looked back and waved, but the woman merely flapped a hand, dismissing her. Ren thought: I wish she hadn't bustled me out so quickly, but she said she would 'do some considering' so perhaps she will help me find Greta. And as she entered the barn that thought gladdened her face.

'You've taken your time,' Lil greeted. 'Steering clear of the mess and the bother of getting her down. And watch your noise. I don't want her woken up.'

'I wouldn't do that.'

'What's that stuff you're carrying?'

'Rabbit stew. It's better than anything.'

'Not if that old hag's turned it out. You can chuck it away.'

'I asked for it specially.'

'Well, I might force it down,' Lil relented, seeing Ren's face.

Handing the plate to her, Ren noticed what Lil had done. She had removed the contents from Ren's rucksack and arranged them upon the barn floor. Ren stared, not knowing how to challenge or to object.

'This looks like business,' Lil commented. She held up Ren's dental groomer.

'You can have it.' Perhaps Lil envied these possessions. 'Take anything you want.'

'I'm fitted out OK, but your kit's a bit short.'

'It wasn't expected I'd be going on a route march.'

Lil laughed and replaced Ren's belongings in the rucksack. 'That's that. Just a routine search.'

Ren decided not to ask her what she was searching for. She wanted to tell her that Annie Gimmer had promised to help them; she wanted to report that the old woman had not seen a patrolman that day.

But her tongue would not work and it was difficult to see Lil through the gauze of approaching sleep. Words were heard indistinctly: 'can't be sure we've shaken him off', and 'move on tonight'.

Then later there was crying, the baby smells of food and nappies. After that her body, still torpid, was hauled into a sitting position and the child thrust on to her lap. She heard: 'We'll strike camp when I've done a reconnaissance. There should be a village not far away, near where I got off the lorry. The driver said it was empty. Now that it's dark, I can check.'

A plastic cape crackled; skirts swirling round trousers created a draught; within the barn's opening, a shape was profiled against the night sky and the voice breathed: 'Found'll probably want a good whinge, but you'll have to prevent it, else she'll be heard.'

And if she were, who might arrive to investigate? Ren asked the empty barn. Would a patrolman appear at the door, swing the beam of his torch across the dirt floor and along walls until it found her struggling in Ren's arms here in this corner, and with its blinding light pin them both down? Or would it be a creature? One whose ears would catch the sound of this miserable crying which could spill out of Found's mouth without need of breath and would not stop however much Ren jogged and rocked. This beast would come sniffing, as the boy had feared, for he knew what fanged things prowled in the darkness, what giants strode from their caves, what ogres sprang from the gullies. In the deserted homesteads Annie had felt the spirits lingering; their peace broken, they would seek out this noise.

But there was nothing Ren could do to silence it. Her soothing whispers were not heard above the interminable wails. As if she, too, sensed danger, the child's clamour grew more desperate; her chest bubbled, her feet kicked and she thrashed to escape the restraint of Ren's grasp. Together they wrestled, while the terrors of the night gathered, invisible. Mouths slavered, clubs were raised, claws were sharpened, fingers were stretched to stitch through hair.

Their noises grew closer. Paws scratched along the rafters. Her head jerked up, Ren saw the hole in the roof. It contracted. A mass leant over the edge. Now it was her throat which shrieked.

'Who's there? Mrs Gimmer, is that you? Mrs Gimmer! Mrs Gimmer!'

The scraping hands vanished and the head which had poked under the roof beam was there no more.

Ren listened for the skid of boots down the wall, the thud of them descending upon the grass, but no sounds reached her above Found's noise. No one could have climbed up there, she told herself. There was nobody. He was just a part of a bad dream.

She managed to loosen her frantic grip upon the baby. She hauled her up to rest against her shoulder and pillowed the head in her palm. 'Nothing and no one shall ever harm you, I promise. I won't let it,' she murmured. What had Annie Gimmer said? 'There's not a deal that'll best you.'

She smiled at the memory; her body became less tense and, made easier, Found gulped; her cries were reduced. Hooped in the sanctuary of Ren's arms, she gradually grew quiet while, steady and alert, Ren stared into the night.

Seven

There was no mistake about the next noises; they crackled the silence that had bound her while the baby slept. Again panic sluiced through her as a stone rattled, as a weight thumped, but she could not escape, make a rush for the doorway with the child tight on her lap. She heard the scrape of a zip being opened, a series of impatient scratches, then, within the tent of a cape, the swaying leaf of a flame.

'Are you awake?' Lil asked. In the light of the match her eyes were bloodshot and shadows pooled her cheeks.

Choked by relief, Ren could not answer.

'I came upon these.' Plunder was tumbled from her anorak: a toy, a cup, candles, a bundle of white towelling, but her voice was not triumphant. 'We'll be glad of the matches. Now we have to shift. Quick.'

'Has someone seen you?'

'Seen me? I can case a joint without being seen.' However, the boast quivered.

'There was . . . I thought there was . . . a person, up there on the roof. I'm not sure.' Ren could not disentangle the sensations; she could not separate the nightmare of the prowling creatures from the huge poking head.

'There's someone about.' The flame shrank along its stalk. 'In one of the cottages . . . there were . . . ashes in the hearth . . . a pan with food in it . . . hadn't had time to grow a mould. We must get out.'

'Perhaps he heard Found crying.'

'I'll strike another match while you pack the buggy.'

'I couldn't stop her.'

'It probably made no difference,' Lil whispered and Ren was grateful to her for not apportioning blame.

She did not because she was too honest. During her search she had discovered that her own competence was not perfect. But pride kept her silent. What she had done had broken the rules of her training, and she was ashamed.

Lil was accustomed to danger, but she had never before undertaken that kind of venture alone. Always she had been accompanied, indeed it was a rule that they reaved in couples or worked in larger teams. Guards and look-outs were necessary. If caught, street people had no rights in law. Unregistered, they had no status. How they were dealt with depended on whim. Yet this night Lil had ignored instruction and practice. She calculated that if the man following them were based in one of the houses, she would discover him before he could her, and she would have no difficulty in making her escape.

Even so, she had not been free of tremors. She was not used to the country night. Roofed by trees, the village lane was a tunnel lit neither by street lamps nor stars. Lil blundered into its verges and cried out at the sudden thrust of a low, searching branch. When, later, her feet slid and stumbled, she thought she walked upon large pebbles until she identified them as cobbles and, as the sky cast a faint sheen upon them, she saw that at last she was in the village street.

Relieved, she leant against a house wall. 'I've walked faster than I thought,' she told herself, because she did not wish to admit it was fear that had caused the trickles of sweat. But these dried up immediately she began to explore. In this kind of terrain she was confident, a skilled pirate; her knowledge was almost instinctive.

The village was not arranged in the kind of geometrical grid she was used to; the buildings were set higgledy-piggledy; the streets, branching at skewed angles, were linked by alleys and sometimes by the walled course of a gill. Nevertheless, Lil was very thorough. Plotting her own points of reference – a flight of scooped steps, a projecting sill, an iron gate – she worked systematically, section by section, and covered every house. Now assisted by stars and the moon-hinting sky, she peered, listened, felt, and she discovered that, although she had brought her tools, she would not need to employ them. When she had selected the houses to enter, she would have no use for jemmy or wrench. At first this did not surprise her; she assumed that looters had already done their work. She even thought, grudgingly: Annie Gimmer has done a good job! But as she continued, her hands examining door jambs, her fingers probing the frames of windows, she realised that none had ever been forced. Because they were not locked.

Lil peered at the knob which had just turned in her hand. She was shocked and confused. For she had never experienced anything comparable to this: houses not yet derelict but left open, perhaps welcoming those without shelter. Usually property was severely guarded, if not with guns and alarms, then with chains, padlocks, wire, bolts. This door inching open frightened her. The cottage had grown sinister. Squeezing herself against the clean-cut stone, all she could hear was her own scraping breath. Her heart drummed.

Eventually, rebuking herself for this weakness, she slid her knife out of a pocket and with it firm in her palm she stepped inside the house. Again she stood, listened. Tense, concentrating, her ears stretched like muscles straining for an object beyond reach, she listened to the silence. And it assailed her, it hammered a way into her head. There it swelled, grew into rhythmic thuds which became like boots that stamped and brought with them the rattle of armaments. Gasping, Lil threw back her arm and swung down the knife in a strong curving stroke. But there were no boots or bullets in that cottage. She had brought their sounds with her. The knife had sliced through empty air.

And its path had run through starlight which laid a feathery illumination at her feet. It showed her a low shelf on which rested, ready to hand, matches and candles. Still trembling with the menace which had invaded her head, Lil grabbed, fumbled; a flame gushed and was transferred to a candle's wick. In its light she saw varnished stone flags, garden pots crammed with soil, a scraggy mattress, a cone of neatly chopped wood beside an iron hearth, a saucepan crusted with soot. There was nothing strange about any of these, except for the gardening pots. It was simply a place used by tramps. What did surprise her was a collection of things arranged tidily upon a piece of old cloth; a baby's dummy, a soft toy so tattered and balding that it was impossible to determine its species, a feeding cup, a drum of dried milk, and squares of white towelling, individually folded, which Lil recognised as old-fashioned nappies. Crooning with pleasure, Lil tightened the belt of her anorak, opened the zip and stuffed her haul into its capacious pouch.

It was only then that she saw the porridge, still moist, in the saucepan and the heavy spade propped by the hearth. And the quiet cottage was again filled with noises but this time they were its own. Lil heard the ring of the pan dropped on to the slate flags as she imagined the owner leaping to face her; she saw him grasp the spade's wooden handle, felt its draught on her shoulder, and heard the crack as the blade cleft through the bone.

She dowsed the flame. The spiral of smoke was invisible but she could smell the melted wax. And she was thinking: Why ever did I light it? I forgot the danger! There's no one I know would have made such a mistake. I put a spotlight on myself for at least two minutes; there's no curtain. I could've been seen for miles.

Then she was out of the cottage, her feet tripped by a boot scraper, snared by tough weeds, gripped by cobbles and twisted in the holes of the crumbling lane. And to the rhythm of her rasping breath, the thought panted: They mustn't find me; I mustn't be caught. But it was not her own safety only that concerned her. If she were captured there would be a search and the others would be discovered. They, too, would be taken. Because of her folly. An unforgivable mistake. She had broken the code of her street people and Lil groaned at the disgrace.

Now, groping over the floor of the barn, she collected the spilled booty and argued to herself that at least she had won this.

'What about Mrs Gimmer?' Ren asked her.

'She's not invited.'

'That wasn't a joke. She said we were to wait till she'd worked something out. I think she was going to help me reach Greta.'

'Well, she's too late. Anyway, we'll be going in the general direction, more or less south. I'll take the buggy this time and you carry Found.'

'I'd like to do that.'

However, the arrangement Lil had chosen had not been in order to give Ren pleasure. It had quite a different purpose. She could discard the buggy, but if she were carrying Found, swift movement would be impeded. Speed and agility are needed for defence.

Eight

Ren had forgotten the weight of the baby. Partially roused as she was laid in the sling, she had agitated them both by her whimpering distress. But snug against Ren's chest and lulled by her movements, Found curled inside her warm hammock and returned to sleep. Then Ren became aware of her load. Her neck was crooked by the pulling fabric and her shoulders ached. But she vowed that she would not complain. In a way, she thought later, she was fortunate to have other things to share her attention.

Under the vaulting hedgerows she was no better at sensing her way than Lil had been earlier, but she put one hand beside Lil's on the buggy and used that as a guide. If it suddenly laboured on grass, they knew they were veering off the lane.

'The lorry driver dropped me somewhere along here, I think,' Lil whispered, 'so I'm hoping we're on the road I came by. I shan't be sure till I see the river. Is that you?'

'What?'

'That noise? Hold it.'

They stopped, but could hear nothing.

'Listen.'

'Is it Found?' Ren suggested as the child's breath suddenly whistled.

'No. It's under the trees. If anyone jumps out, you lie down. I don't want to be punching the wrong one. So stay clear. Safe.'

Safe! Ren thought: I haven't been safe since I left the living-work unit. Now she and Lil were not only in flight but must be ready for ambush. 'What did you do, Lil?' she whispered. The question was possible in the dark; she could not see Lil's face.

'*Do?* I didn't do anything. I'm a street person. That's enough. Scum. Security are after you on the streets yet they'll not let you be if they find you trying to get out. It's their way of enjoying themselves.'

'I see.' Ren asked no more questions. She was thinking: When they did reports on the news screen about street people, they never said anything like that.

They had not walked far before the nature of the darkness altered. Low by the roadside it distilled into mist, and gradually this took on a modest lustre which reflected a change in the sky.

'It's the river,' Lil whispered, relieved, and it guided them forward, steamed under them when they crossed over it and continued at their side.

'That's the two bridges. I remember them. In a mile or two there should be a railway line. Keep your eyes skinned for it.'

'Why?'

'We'll walk down the tracks.'

'What about the trains?'

'The lorry driver told me the line's been closed years.'

'I seem to be seeing more,' Ren murmured later.

'Soon be dawn.'

It came gently, a soft tendril uncurling at their feet. Hunched over their burdens, they watched the lane's tarmac pale and grow level and smooth for their surer steps. Beside them, the steam sheeting the river slunk under branches and showed them water foamed by boulders and sliding over great tablets of rock. There, fixed by one of them, they saw a post with a point, a swelling, grey, a stirring, feathers – a bird. It rose languidly, flapped broad wings and led their eyes upward over the trees and into the opal sky.

And they saw in front of them, seemingly not far away, a line of arches. Though strange in this landscape, they were not alien. Their curves had the grace of rocks eroded by waterfalls and their stones were fluted by rain. They were massive yet slender; they hoisted the sky's weight with ease upon their huge shoulders and windowed the hesitant light.

'That's a facer!' Lil murmured.

'What is it?'

'A viaduct. To take the railway line.'

'I can't walk on top of that! I just can't,' Ren said. She was hungry; pain screamed in her neck; her legs were buckling. And she could look no longer. Turning her eyes away, she confessed, 'I'll be dizzy. I'll fall off.'

'You'll steady up after a rest,' Lil stated, brisk. 'We'll try that wood,' and without further deliberation, she left the road and led Ren across a field until they reached a dense plantation of firs.

Ren saw no significance in Lil's quick decision. As she mixed Found's feed, using water Lil had taken from the river, and as she opened tins for themselves while the baby was fed, all she could think of was sleep. She made no comment when Lil announced, 'Before it's fully daylight I'll have a scout round. Join you two in a quick shut-eye when I come back.'

Lil was pleased not to be questioned. She, too, was drugged by fatigue. Therefore it suited her to be relieved of the effort of explanation.

There's no proof I spotted it, she argued to herself. A head, shoulders, above the parapet of the viaduct. The minute Ren looked away. Her telling about a head poking through the barn roof has started me seeing visions. With a line round the head, perhaps the hard brim of a cap. It could've been a mirage like Great-great-grandpa met soldiering in the desert.

Lil hoped that it was, because if the watcher were the man

pursuing them, she considered that it was her fault he was there. He could have seen her light in the cottage. He could have gone ahead of her to the barn and frightened Ren. Then, afterwards, all he had to do was wait until they came out and follow them.

Why, when he's so close, doesn't he jump on us? she asked wearily. I'd welcome a straight fight. He's one of those sadists, waiting for us to crack. Well, he'll have a long wait. Because we shan't.

Refreshed by a short nap after her breakfast, the baby soon woke Ren. Shoulders throbbing, sleep misting her eyes, she groped for the buggy and lifted the baby out. Immediately the wailing ceased. This was flattering; it suggested a developing skill. Perhaps she could learn how to play with her. She sat Found on the sleeping-bag and, after tickling her in the ribs, wondered what to do next. Thus preoccupied she did not see the boy until he stood beside her.

He grinned at her sharp cry. 'You've got a frog's jump!'

'How did you know we were here?'

'Looked.' He returned the baby's stare. 'What sort is it, then?'

'A girl. We call her Found.'

'Look at that sticking-out chin. Aren't girls supposed to be pretty?'

'She is. More than I am.' Ren was sorry she had said that. It might prompt the boy to think that she was ugly.

He examined her dispassionately. 'I don't think so. I like your brown eyes and you'll look better with all your side teeth. There's not a deal more I can see under the dirt.'

'Who's talking!'

'Dirt's useful. I leave this for camouflage.' Seeing Ren stroke a shoulder when she laughed, he asked, 'Was she heavy in that sling?'

'You bet. Try her.'

The boy put out his hands, paused and replaced them in his

pockets. 'She might cry,' he excused himself.

'She's always pulling her lips together like that. I don't think it means she doesn't like you.'

He made a grimace. 'No matter. Look, I've fetched her some milk. Mrs Gimmer's boiled it, she says you're to know. So it keeps longer.'

'She gave me a dish of stew yesterday.'

'Rabbit or partridge?'

'Rabbit.'

'I can't decide which I like best.' He sighed, dreaming. 'Only she'd run out of stew this morning.'

Ren did not like to confess that she and Lil had been given the last of it. 'I wish I could have stew at Mrs Gimmer's every day.'

'I don't have it every day. I used to live with her all the time, but I don't any more. Here, I brought these.'

He held out a screw of fabric that might have been the remnant of a vest. Ren saw soft globes each made of tiny beads that were polished and fat. Some had split and oozed a magenta juice.

'What are they?'

His mouth gaped. 'You don't know? Blackberries. Try a taste.'

Hesitantly, she took one, rolled it over her tongue and squashed it warily between her teeth. 'That's lovely.' Her eyes filled. Once it had been her mother who had given her small treats. 'May I have another?'

''Course. There's plenty more by the river. Would she fancy one?'

'The seeds might stick in her throat.'

'Her throat's wide as this dale! I've heard her yell.' But he deferred to Ren's caution and pressing two of the berries in his palm, he produced a rich nectar. 'Here, have a lick of this,' he commanded and pushed the tip of a finger against Found's lips. She sucked it in, accepted it again then, her nostrils flaring with disgust, she opened her mouth and let the juice drip away.

'She doesn't waste time showing her mind on a matter,' he admired. Then Found leant forward and emitted a long, growling fart.

'Just listen to that!' the boy exclaimed, delighted. But Found had not finished. She had at her command a whole arsenal, some small shot rattling out, some fast bursting grenades and, after tense seconds of waiting as the flame on the fuse raced towards the gunpowder, a deep rumbling explosion. The boy knelt beside her and, puffing out his face, attempted to compete. Until at last Found lost interest, drew her performance to a close with a modest hiss and yawned. As they stopped laughing, the boy said, 'She could teach Mrs Gimmer a thing or two,' and Ren told him, 'Lil's coming.'

The boy rose. 'Blinking hell, I near forgot!' He began to unfasten the buckles on his pack and paid no attention to Lil until, reaching him, she demanded, 'Who're you?'

'I could ask the same.'

She regarded him, judged his power and weight, calculated that her own were superior, and drew her hand out of her pocket, empty. 'How did you get here?'

'Walked. There isn't much call for charabancs in these parts.'

'What do you want?'

'Will you lay off? Do I look like a patrolman?'

'You might do jobs for them.'

The boy's lips flickered. 'They'd never have me.' He stared at the place where Lil's knife was hidden. 'I don't own the tackle.'

Lil flinched. 'Curse you. Who told you I did?'

'I don't need telling. But Mrs Gimmer warned me it wouldn't be a hankie you'd be stretching for.'

'Her? That old witch? You're in with her?' Her lips tight, it seemed that Lil might leap at him, forgo her weapon and squeeze his throat in her fists.

The boy stepped back, lifted his shoulders and sized Lil up. 'I don't know what you mean, but it sounds nasty.'

Ren intervened: 'Mrs Gimmer sent him. With more milk for—'

'So he's her errand boy.' The scorn was corrosive.

'No. I'm her son. Adopted. Just watch your mouth.'

'And what's happened to hers?' Lil shrieked, pointing at Found. Without turning her back on the boy, she slid over to Found and tilted the baby's face. 'What's this on her chin? Has she sicked up?' Then she saw the juice-sodden rag, a few remaining berries and the lees of pulp. For a moment she was rendered speechless, before: 'You fools. You ignorant, dim-witted, clod-headed fools. Pushing blackberries on her! Raw! She's a baby, not an experiment. You wouldn't like it if someone got a handful of blackberries and stuffed them in your mouth.'

'We didn't. It was only the juice,' Ren stuttered.

'I wouldn't say no,' the boy told her. 'Save me the trouble of picking them first. Now if you've got a minute, I'll hand this over.' He had unravelled the straps of his pack and now levered out a small box and swung it by the handle set into the lid. In each of the sides was a pane of transparent material that looked brittle and was yellowed with smoke. Behind these was a candle. 'You light it through this little door,' he instructed.

'Don't teach me how to light a lantern!' Lil snapped.

'Mrs Gimmer's sent it. "And you tell them," she said, "my advice is go through the tunnel."'

'Why?'

'Ask her. I'm only the errand boy.'

Ren said, 'I don't want to go by a tunnel.' She imagined it, a pipe resounding with footsteps which ceased when you paused to listen but started immediately you walked on.

Lil, too, appeared to have her own fears. Her mood had changed;

her hostility was suspended. She stared away from the boy and stood taut, her fingers twisting the fabric of a skirt. 'A tunnel's a death trap. There's no escape. You can be picked off as you come out. I didn't ask for advice.'

'You don't have to take it.'

'It could be a trick.'

'She's not a body to play tricks. You've got traps and tricks on the brain.'

'I have cause.'

For a moment he was silent, then he said quietly, 'You'd not be seen in the tunnel.'

That was true, and Lil thought: Shall we risk it? 'Is it a shorter way?' she asked.

'Quicker than tramping over the moor.'

'I hadn't squared up to tunnels.'

Or viaducts. She regarded the boy. He was short, skinny. Would she have seen his head so far away? And he was not wearing a cap, but he may have tucked that out of sight. Was he the person who had been spying on them? Carefully she composed a question: 'Do you ever walk along it, the viaduct?'

'You wouldn't catch me on that. It's years since it was seen to. I reckon any moment it could come crashing down.'

He had found nothing suspicious about the question. Lil said to herself: He wasn't lying; it wasn't this one that was up there behind the parapet this morning.

She said, 'When I've fitted in a kip, we might give that tunnel a try.' She tried to ignore Ren's frightened face.

'Do you want to hear a short cut to it?' He pointed through the trees, described landmarks: a diminutive waterfall, a stile, a ruined farmhouse, a pine uprooted by a gale, a bridge, the railway line and the cutting which led to the tunnel's mouth.

'Thanks. What's your name?'

'More of the catechism! Nowadays Mrs Gimmer calls me Brocket.' Lil's expression told him that she did not know what a brocket was, that she knew nothing about young stags. So he added, 'I like that much more than Knobber.' His lips controlled a smile as her curiosity took the bait.

'Why?'

'A brocket's a bit older and his antlers have got more prongs.'

Nine

He sat in the cutting by the entrance to the tunnel, not too close and hidden by shrubs. He wanted to be sure they had followed his directions correctly, but he had not calculated that he would wait all morning; he had forgotten that Lil had planned to take a nap.

There were other things he could be doing, he rebuked himself. He could be picking more blackberries or checking on Mrs Gimmer's snares. He could not lay them himself; he could not deliberately set out to catch a rabbit, but if there were one caught and not wriggling too much, he would take it, find Mrs Gimmer and hang about till it was cooked.

'You're not trying to save my legs but fill your belly,' she would scold, and she was right. 'Now you buzz off,' she would say when he had eaten, 'and have a good tramp.' By that she meant: I can't be doing with you any longer; I'm too old to spend vigour on charity; keep out of my way a fair bit.

He did so because he would not impose upon her. Had she not found him right at the start? Fed him and tried to teach him some of her lore. He had told Ren that someone had dumped Found as people dump dogs they grow tired of, but she was not the first baby that had been dumped.

In a moment he would crawl from this hiding-place and have a look round. He had not undertaken to do that; they were not expecting him to be standing guard, but he had decided he should. He suspected that this was no ordinary chase.

There had been something peculiar about it right from the start. It worried him; he could not sort it out. Brocket went through the reasons.

That's the baby, where I picked her up. He selected a pine cone and placed it between his feet. It's a mystery who left her in that particular place. Next morning there's a patrolman down on the road and they bolt with her out of the cave. He moved the cone an inch. There's nothing new in that; I've watched.

But the man didn't do this. Brocket's hand leapt forward. The cone was nipped between pincer fingers. That's the second mystery. He had chances enough. They went down the dale, then side of the river to the railway line. Brocket pushed the cone in a neat loop and walked his fingers behind it.

Questions: Why didn't he pounce? Why didn't he corner them in the barn? It's child's play, easier than running down a one-legged grouse. Brocket scraped at the earth, laid the cone in the nest he had made and dangled a twig over it.

And another thing. Why haven't I clapped eyes on him? He's a good tracker. Better than me, he admitted, and covered the twig with leaves.

It was time to do a check. He inched on his belly to the top of the cutting and crouched in the protection of a hazel whose leaves yellowed the slope. He examined the ground thoroughly. A good distance away, the long dyke of the mountain showed nothing unusual; on the crest of the moor behind him, no watching shape was added to the silhouette of the crags. Beneath him, driven deep through the granite rock was the tunnel.

Brocket held his breath, listening. In the air above him the decayed branch of a sycamore creaked, a magpie clappered, but the sounds that came to his ears from the tunnel's dark mouth were the clang of alarm bells, the screech of tearing timbers, the thud of crashing rocks, the cries which shrilled before they were stifled by the black foaming dust.

'That didn't stop the building of it,' Mrs Gimmer had said. 'After they had opened it up again and dragged the men out. They carried them away, along this road the Romans built for a different purpose, and buried them here. They didn't lay them in the regular churchyard; they placed them under this wall.' The graves were no more than humps, hardly bending the grass. 'But if they'd been lowered into that pothole, they'd not have stayed from their wandering. It was a bad death they had, and they rise up at the right season and go back where they ended to mourn. You can hear them. The groans, the lamentations. By those that keep them in memory, they can be heard.'

Brocket discovered that his body was shaking and his hands were over his ears until gradually he realised that the sounds he could hear were the whines of a baby and the crunch of clinkers under the buggy wheels. He watched the girls pause as Lil lit the lantern. Their faces were white, showing fatigue. Or possibly fear. He could sympathise with that. Nothing would have induced him to enter the tunnel and risk the sight of its ghosts. He waited until the girls had vanished then he slid down the bank and ran back. It was rare that he ventured so close to this tunnel, and neither did anyone else who knew of its dead and 'kept them in memory'. Thinking of this, Brocket sensed that in some way it was important but he had gone a good distance before he understood.

He halted and tried it out: A patrolman wouldn't be scared. He wouldn't know what he might meet there. His ears wouldn't catch the moaning. So he wouldn't be put off.

Now Mrs Gimmer told the girls to walk down it. She reckoned that would put stop to anyone following.

That means she suspects it's a person who knows the story. A fellow who keeps the dead 'in memory'. One who'd fight shy of the place.

The upshot of that is, she reckons the chaser isn't a patrolman,

Brocket argued. She calculates he lives on these fells.

He paused, shocked at the notion, then continued relentlessly. And there's more to it than that. If she's got top and bottom of it, she knows who the man is. Only she's too frail to jump out on him and scare him away.

So what does she do? She sends me with a lantern and issues out the message, and says to me, 'Stir yourself, young Brocket. Be of some use. Never you pay heed to that bossyboots; there's things she can learn.'

He thought over his reasoning. However, there was something about it that was not quite right. Mrs Gimmer was assuming that the hunter would give up at the tunnel and turn back.

But surely they could not rely on that? Surely he would not be put off when he had followed the girls right from the cave? He, Brocket, had suppressed his fear of the tunnel long enough to spend a morning by its entrance, so it was unlikely that this person could not do the same. And if he dared not follow them into it, wouldn't he make a detour round it and when it finished, continue along the open track? That is what he, Brocket, would do. He could be right on their heels.

And he had turned, was running over bridges and stepping-stones, was leaping stiles and gills, pushing through a plantation, taking the steep ascent of the slopes at breath-rasping speed. Racing by the side of the tunnel as it burrowed under the moor, Brocket blocked his ears to the sounds, the groans and lamentations, that whistled drearily from the air shafts; he closed his mind to the sights they conjured, telling himself that it was clumsiness that made his feet slither and jarred his back by a fall. He tried to concentrate on another puzzle, a new question. It was: Why should a man who is not a patrolman set out to pursue these homeless girls? They were no business of his. They were doing no harm.

And fighting for breath, his chest pounding, he at last knew the answer. It burst in his head and stayed there, refusing to be dislodged. He was convinced by it. He was as sure of it as he was of the mountain at his shoulder and the tunnel under his feet. Appalled, his skin already sticky with sweat, Brocket knew that it was not Ren or Lil that this person was after. It was the baby he sought.

Having emerged from the tunnel, Lil and Ren bumped the push-chair further along the track and forced it round embankments before reaching another viaduct. Longer than the first, it paced ahead of them on elegant stilts.

'I can't walk much further,' Ren said. She expected some objection, but Lil nodded.

'We'll take a rest soon.' Then she saw Brocket. 'Just look who's in the rear! Why couldn't he lend a hand with this buggy?' But her tone changed as soon as he reached them and she saw his face. She warned, 'Keep up that pace and you'll rupture a lung. Come under one of the arches.'

So they squashed together, their backs against the damp masonry of the viaduct, and waited until Brocket had recovered his breath.

He began, 'It's like this. I reckon the man after you is not one of those patrolmen; he lives on the fells. I reckon he knows all about what has happened here, because . . .' and then he halted. He realised that if he carried on he would have to mention Mrs Gimmer and explain that she guessed who their pursuer was. He could not do that. He could not bring Mrs Gimmer into it. Lil would accuse her of some kind of conspiracy. He would not have that said about the woman who had acted as a mother to him, replacing the one he did not even recall.

'What makes you say that?' Lil prompted.

He struggled to circle the difficulty. 'Any regular patrolman would have lost you by now, the route you've taken.'

'You haven't.'

'I live here. How many times have you spotted me?'

She did not answer.

'How many times have you spotted *him*?'

'I haven't counted. Once outside the cave. I didn't fancy getting close, but he looked a tall man. Hefty. Ren thought she saw a head at the roof of the barn. We've heard noises, too: when we were on the lane last night. And there was someone on the viaduct this morning.'

'You thought it was me!'

Annoyed by his grin, Lil resolved that he should not hear how she had entered a cottage and foolishly lit a candle.

Brocket argued, 'All that's against him being a patrolman. They don't lounge about on a road when their target's a spitting distance away. They don't climb on to barn roofs. Why hasn't he rounded you up?'

Lil ignored this, pretending to be absorbed in licking the hem of one of her skirts and wiping Found's face. But her fingers were less deft than usual. All day she had puzzled over this question and it filled her with unease.

'I've seen them,' he insisted. 'They don't waste time.'

'No need to remind me of that.' Her voice had altered. It quivered, low.

But Brocket paid no attention to its horror. He repeated, 'So why hasn't this chap made a grab? I'll tell you. Because he's not interested in you. He's after that baby. That's what he wants.'

They stared at him. They were unable to assimilate his words. Until, her voice cracking, Ren asked, 'Why?'

'I don't know.' He had done what he had hoped. Somehow he had managed not to implicate Annie Gimmer.

Finally Lil stated, 'You're mad. Just say he *is* a dalesman. What makes you think he's after the baby more than us? What's stopping him trying a grab?'

70

'He's come close. Ren thinks she saw him at the roof of the barn.'

'I screamed for Annie Gimmer.'

'That would put him off,' Brocket argued. 'He's biding his time, waiting till the right moment.'

The child had begun to whine and grumble. Lil held her to a shoulder and tapped her back. 'Why should a chap on the fells want a baby? Who'd want this bother?'

It was such a sensible question that Brocket felt foolish. It made his deductions seem ridiculous.

'It's time Found was cleaned up.' Lil had dismissed his speculations. 'I won't use one of the pads, they're giving her an itch, so I'll try a terry towelling nappy for a change. Lucky we've got them.' She removed a bundle from the push-chair and lifted up a square of white.

Ren stroked the soft looped fabric. 'I haven't seen these before.'

'Lit on them in the cottage. They're the sort babies used to have. You don't throw them away, you wash them.'

'Weren't they funny things to leave, Lil?'

'Why?' There was a squeak of plastic and immediately a pungent smell.

'I'm wondering what's happened to the baby.'

Lil shrugged uninterested.

Puzzled, Ren continued, 'If there was a baby, the nappies would go with it, wouldn't they? You wouldn't find any nappies if there was no baby about.'

Brocket asked, 'What cottage?'

'One in the village.'

'They're all empty.'

'That shows how much you know,' she snapped. 'Someone had been in it not so long back. It had porridge in a pan in the hearth. And candles and matches. And a baby's dummy, and a battered old doll, and a feeding cup and a tin of dried milk.'

'Strikes me that someone's been getting ready to look after a baby.'

He could not see the expression on Lil's face but her movements were arrested. She was completely still. A sigh like a lament came from Ren's direction. Found was quiet, as if waiting for conclusions to be made.

'I didn't think of that,' Lil muttered. She hated to make the admission. She had decided that the candles had been part of the trick of leaving the door unlocked, that possibly they had been left to tempt her to show a light. She had not questioned whether the rest of her plunder had any significance.

'Patrolmen don't store nappies and dummies and suchlike in deserted cottages on the off-chance they might hit upon an abandoned baby; but a dalesman might leave the stuff handy when he was planning to make a grab,' Brocket insisted.

'I think Brocket's right,' Ren was obliged to say although she did not like to disagree with Lil.

'And what if he is? What difference does it make?' But Lil knew her question was superfluous. Before this, their adversary had been an intelligible figure and she had known what to expect. Now he was inexplicable; he belonged to a region that was foreign to her and was compelled by a sinister purpose. This was not a contender for whom she had been trained.

Dejected, she added, 'All we can do is keep ahead of him.' She searched through her skirts, found a safety-pin and screwed it into Found's clean nappy.

'If we could get her to Greta . . .' Ren tried.

Lil said, 'We can't think of that till we've shook this chap off.'

'I'll go back and search round,' Brocket decided.

'You don't know the target.'

'I know it's not a patrolman. So I'll look in different places, the crannies they don't know exist. I might find out whether the person is walking round the tunnel.' He thought that Mrs Gimmer would approve.

Lil nodded. 'I suppose there's nothing to lose.'

'I'll take you where you won't be seen, first,' Brocket said and, meeting no objection, he put his hand on the push-chair and heaved it over the boggy grass.

Ten

They had not gone far before they saw him. The girls had crouched by a shallow stream while Brocket checked the road they must cross, then as he led them over it, they saw a figure lift above a slight rise. And although this was the crisis they had imagined, they were unprepared. They halted, their breath held and bodies tense.

Brocket whispered, 'Let's make a run for it.'

Lil's answer was to drag Found out of the sling and thrust her upon Ren. 'No chance,' she hissed, judging the distance between them, and her hand went for her knife. 'We have to make a stand. You guard those two.'

The figure drew nearer, waved and quickened his pace.

'It's no more than a boy,' Brocket murmured and their breaths gushed out.

'Hello there!' the person shouted.

'What is he?' Ren gasped, and her wonder was shared.

For the stranger, not much taller than Lil, was festooned with equipment. A rolled-up tent was balanced across his shoulders; a hard hat like a fireman's helmet bobbed at his nape; looped round his neck was a thick rope and over it dangled a pair of binoculars; maps were slung from his waist. Underneath all that his clothing was neat, with no tear or blemish, and his boots were of strong leather polished a gleaming brown.

'Where are you making for?' he asked Brocket. Then he saw Ren behind him and the baby in her arms. His mouth gaping, he caught sight of the knife point at the base of Lil's fist and sprang back. His eyes swept across their barrier as he calculated whether he had room to escape. Then he took a deep breath, assumed an expression suitable for combat, slipped his binoculars over his head and swung them from the strap. 'Who's first? You?' he addressed Lil. 'Or can you only fight in threes?'

'We don't want a fight,' Ren said.

'Depends,' Lil qualified and challenged the boy with: 'Do you live near here?'

He shook his head. 'I've only been here four days. No, five, if you count the day I arrived.'

Impatient with this scrupulous answer, Lil demanded, 'So how come you can just – ' she nodded towards his equipment and to the wide country around them, ' – just walk about?'

'Why shouldn't I?'

'You're not an absconder, then?'

'Of course not.'

'Then I reckon you're working for the patrolmen,' she concluded, a menace in her voice.

The boy's astonishment almost equalled that on seeing the baby. 'I don't work for anyone. I'm freelance.'

'Doing what?'

'Studying this region.'

His answer was so preposterous, so out of tune with their danger and flight, so free of terrors, that they were speechless. At last Brocket's laugh expressed their relief. The others joined him and Found spun out a skein of bubbles.

The boy blushed. 'Now I have given you a laugh, I'll say goodbye.'

Before Ren could offer the apology she intended, Brocket had asked, 'What're you studying it for?'

'What *for*?' The question disconcerted him.

76

'I've been studying it for years.' Brocket considered it necessary not to be outclassed.

'It's not only the geology I'm interested in,' the boy confided as to another enthusiast. 'It's the evidence of habitations as well, as far back as I can find.'

'I can tell you about them.'

'I'd appreciate it if you would. Also, there's a henge I'm looking for.' He began to unfold a map.

'We haven't time for prattle about habitations; we've got our own to find,' Lil interrupted.

'A henge is more of a site, sort of religious,' he corrected diligently.

'Is it now? Have you seen anyone?'

The boy frowned. 'I think I have. Now where was I? Do you want the grid reference?'

'I hope you aren't being sarcastic.'

'Why should I be?' He was totally mystified. 'Don't you carry a map?'

'Oh, forget it!' (Later she commented to the others: 'It was just our luck to run into a loony.') 'Who was this bloke?'

'The person I met? Was it a man?' he asked himself. 'No. As far as I recall it was a woman.'

'Annie Gimmer? Was she really old?' Brocket asked.

'She didn't give her name, and I cannot possibly deduce her age. She asked if I'd seen a little one in a green jacket.' He peered for colours under the dirt and addressed Ren. 'I suppose she meant you.'

'Someone looking for me! It could be Madge.' She felt dizzy; her arms seemed as if they would snap under Found's weight. Contrary to Madge's order, she had left the cave and rescue had passed by.

Brocket and Lil said nothing; each was working out the significance of this mischance.

The stranger regarded them, puzzled. 'I'm afraid she didn't mention where you could find her. At least, I don't remember. We talked for a while about other things.'

'What things?'

'There are quite a number besides making appointments to meet,' he answered Lil tartly. 'Goats, for a start. Sheep, too, and what happens at lambing.'

Again they stared at him, incredulous. Lil said, 'Sounds nice. It's a pity we haven't time to hear about them. We need to get off this road.'

He nodded and bent his head over the map. 'It's not a terribly convenient moment for me, either.'

('I could've throttled him,' Lil said when they were back on their path; 'all he was interested in was his rotten old map.')

Feeling her glare, the stranger looked up, regarded her for a moment, then his eyes rested on Found. Bored and fretful, she was struggling as Lil fitted her back in the sling. 'I'd say what you need at the moment is a little coup,' he commented. 'They were used to drag feed over rough ground and had runners like sleighs. I've seen diagrams.'

Brocket laughed and gestured towards their buggy and packs. 'You can lend us a tractor and trailer if you've got a spare.'

'Come on,' Lil urged. 'If you meet a chap asking questions, you haven't seen us. And we haven't got this baby. Understand?'

'Not really. But so far I've met only that woman.'

'Well, remember – you'd be sorry if you squealed.' Then they left him, forcing the buggy over the stones and bracken, but Ren ran back and whispered, 'If you see her again, that woman who was looking for me, or another one called Greta, please tell her you've seen me. She's promised to collect me. I'm Ren, and they are Brocket and Lil. What's your name?'

'Hilary. Won't she need to know your route?' However, Ren had already gone.

Resuming his walk, he said to himself: One issues threats and the other makes a request. Added to which, the lot of them are roaming about without a map. Dad would have been dumbfounded. The height of folly he would have called it. 'It's essential to have everything planned,' he would say; 'equipment, food, route, down to the last tittle. I'll take you up to the dales, give you a good grounding, start you off. It won't be long before I'm well enough to go back.' But he never was.

'I liked him,' Brocket said, unconsciously fuelling Lil's irritation.

'Who was he? What's this freelance?'

'I would've liked his tent and some of that rope,' Brocket murmured.

'He's all style and no innards. There's no mud on his boots.'

'He keeps them polished, that's why. Next time I go down to the service station, I'm going to look whether there's any like them waiting to be pinched.'

'Just sauntering about! Not a care,' she described, envious.

Lil's grumbles continued but Brocket did not interrupt them. He saw no reason why the boy should be interested in their problems; indeed, he was relieved that he had not asked about them. Brocket was tired of questions. What interested him was the boy's business. Or pastime. He did not know which it was. But to walk the fells with a purpose was intriguing; it might even be exciting to do this studying, as the boy called it, to use maps, compare what you found with the illustrations in books. He had seen one or two of those in abandoned cottages but had been disappointed to find few contained pictures and he was put off by their mouldy smell.

'I wouldn't mind having a try at that,' he told Ren.

'At what?'

'Roving the fells with ropes hanging off you, and a sound tent – not a rickety one in tatters – and with leather boots on, and having it all tidy in your mind, what's what.'

'Why?'

'It'd be something to do.' His enthusiasm was dashed by her listlessness. Then at last he understood the reason for it and for her pinched face.

'That Madge won't have given up, Ren.' He wanted to prevent the tears from swilling down.

'I don't expect she'll carry on looking. Or the person she sends.' Sliding a hand into a pocket, Ren sieved the stones through her fingers. There were six. 'They can't do it for ever.'

'Of course they'll keep looking. They'll not go back till they've found you.'

'If they find us, so can the hunter.'

'There's something in that,' he admitted. 'Only your person'll be in the open, not like him, so we'll see her. And Mrs Gimmer's got eyes in her head like a hawk. She'll see her and pass on the word,' he encouraged, and was gratified by Ren's smile.

Walking ahead of them, he dragged the buggy through gaps between blocks of rock, not high but paving the ground as far as Ren could see. White-mottled and deeply fissured, they were bald of vegetation until they narrowed to form a long causeway and were scattered with trees. With their roots searching down the cracks for sustenance, the trees were misshapen, angular, almost bare for the winter months.

'We aren't stopping here,' Brocket told them. 'Those ashes don't give shelter and you can't rest easy on those clints. Further up there's a cowhouse.'

'I could've done without the tree sprouting out of the roof,' Lil said when they reached it but added, 'I bet that clever dick on the road couldn't find this on his map.' She smiled at Brocket to suggest he should receive her remark as a compliment.

Inside, they stood and shivered, no longer warmed by the

walking, chilled by the whistling draughts.

'Mother forgot to pack my gloves,' Ren said.

Two days earlier Lil would have mocked this dependence. Now she promised, 'We'll find something.'

'We're in for a frost,' Brocket warned. 'But you can't chance a fire. The smoke'd be seen across the whole dale. I'm going, use the daylight that's left.'

'Shan't you be hungry?' Ren asked.

'I've some oat cakes from Mrs Gimmer. I've just thought – I could try laying a false trail. I'd want a few things of hers.' He nodded towards Found.

Lil took out her knife, examined the buggy and prised off a length of plastic trim; Ren spooned the last measure of feed into Found's bottle and handed him the empty drum.

'I'll not go far wrong with these,' he said.

They were standing in one half of the building, in the open chamber where the tree grew and rabbit holes pocked the soft floor. On the other side of a partition built to waist height was the second part of the shippon; it was designed to hold the cows. A gangway ran down its centre and on each side of that, separated by posts and barriers of short planks, were the stalls. Brocket caught Ren's eye and stabbed a thumb towards one of them.

As she joined him, he announced loudly to suggest he was showing her over the premises: 'They milked the cows in these stalls.' Then, in a whisper: 'Look, Mrs Gimmer gave this me years ago.' He fumbled under his jersey and drew a thong of leather over his head. On it was threaded a small hoop. 'Farmers used to hang them up in the byres, so as no harm would come.'

'What is it?' She was afraid they would be heard.

'A witch stone. It's for scaring them off. The hole has to be bored by water, Mrs Gimmer says.'

She held it in her palm and examined the tiny perfectly rounded window sunk in its centre. 'I hadn't thought about witches.' She did not confess that at first she had imagined Annie Gimmer was one.

'Best to be on the safe side.'

The stone was smooth, a milk colour tinged with rose; in the half-light of the cow stall it shone a faint satin through rubbing against his chest. Ren thought she had never seen anything so lovely.

'Won't you need it?'

'You take it. There's Found, too, and someone, something, we don't know what, is after her.'

So she looped the thong round her neck and felt the stone slide under her jersey, unexpectedly warm against her skin.

When Brocket had gone, Ren confessed, 'I don't like this cow place. I wish it was smaller. I wish the door at the end of the stalls hadn't fallen off. We can be seen.'

'No different from the barn,' Lil reminded her, 'but I can tell you, staying put gives me the jitters.' She did not believe that their pursuer would have been defeated by the tunnel; she could not persuade herself that Brocket's strategy of leaving a false trail would work. 'The other one can catch up.'

'We mustn't go till Brocket comes back,' Ren pleaded and was only partially satisfied by Lil's answer: 'We'll take stock tomorrow.'

They raked over the floor and fed the baby. They changed her and using some orange juice from the store in the buggy they washed her bottom; they dressed her in a clean suit and another jacket against the increasing cold. When they had finished attending to her, Lil said, 'Your turn now,' and cut holes in a pair of socks to improvise mittens.

However, occupation busied their hands only. It could not distract their thoughts. Making a neat row of the tins, both noticed how short it was; dressing Found, they both saw that she was dirty, that the folds of her throat were sticky with food and that she was patched with an irritant rash. But they did not remark on any of these things. Nor, when their tasks were ended and the daylight had receded, did they give words to their sense of an imminent threat.

They arranged their sleeping-bags in the larger chamber where the tree grew through the rafters, its branches fanned against the night sky. They lay down with Found between them and watched the peaty motes settle round them in the dusk and a deeper night enter the stalls, but they did not express their fear. Ren's was: Brocket said, someone, *something*, is after Found. Lil's was: If it really is a fellman hunting us, will he have made a deal with Security to turn me in? And they did not admit that they both were in readiness, for neither had removed her shoes.

But their goodnights were: 'There isn't much wind; we shall hear,' and: 'I've got my ears pinned back,' and: 'So have I.'

Thus they listened, but they did not know for whom.

Eleven

Their wait did not seem long but afterwards Ren decided it had probably been several hours. She remembered she had closed her eyes in order to listen more comfortably and supposed she must have dozed off. When she opened her eyes again she thought for a moment that it was daytime, then she realised that the chamber was lit by the moon. It splashed into the broken roof and through the tree's branches which made filigree shadows on the bright floor. She heard Lil whisper, 'There's something. I'm going outside. Stay with Found. Take this.' Her hand was lifted and her fingers were pressed round a knife's haft.

Ren knelt with one hand cupping Found's head, the other clutching Lil's knife. She did not consider how she might use the weapon. All she knew was the blood thundering in her ears and the blade cold against her palm.

'I've done a complete circuit and turned up nothing,' Lil reported. 'Must have heard that tree scraping against a tile. But on the opposite fell, there's a light. I have to climb up there, to check.'

'Shall we all go?' Ren wished she could control her voice; it was always tight and thin when she was frightened.

'We can't heave Found about on a recce. There's no danger here. If it'd make you feel better, you can keep the knife.'

Ren made a noise, gruff, and was not sure whether it was to mean refusal or acceptance.

Lil was zipping up her body warmer, pulling on gloves. 'It's a lot colder, really sharp. Be back soon.'

There was a pad of footsteps and the crunch of dried twigs. That was all. The tiny sounds rippled the silence, then it settled again, heavy and ominous in the vast depths of the night.

At least I can see; the moon never came into the cave, Ren argued to herself, trying to be bold. But beyond the dazzle of moonlight, the night lay colourless, something that was guessed but not known; within its deep folds could lurk an invisible menace. And she realised that, sitting in the trough of light, she could be seen as clearly as if it were day. Immediately, her fingers crippled with panic, she tore off Found's rugs and crawled with her into the shadows at the base of the tree. Half-roused, the child coughed and began a confused whimpering and for a moment this and Ren's soothing breaths were the night's only sounds. Then gradually she thought she heard others, heard the darkness spawning small creaks of wood, pin-point clinks of metal, brief cracks of stiff fabric. She held her breath, her mind begging the noises to cease. They did so momentarily, then were replaced by scratching against planks, the suck of a mass heaved up, the slither of boots somewhere among the cow stalls, along the passage, and then the thud of them on the floor of the wide mew. They hesitated at the edge of the light's shaft; and, her jaws clamped against screams, Ren felt the darkness expand, shudder, split open and disgorge in horrible slow motion first the boots, then trousers, layers of jacket, muffler, waterproof cape, and finally a cap pulled round a face which showed spectral under the white moon. Talon fingers came up and shaded the eyes; they peered into Ren's corner. 'I can see you. You've no call to hide,' the voice cajoled.

It belonged to a woman.

Ren did not move. Clutched to her, the child's body pressed Brocket's gift hard against her chest. 'I've got something that turns away witches,' her breath siffled.

The mouth was drawn open again; a tongue could be seen between broken teeth. 'I'm no witch. I shan't hurt you.'

'What are you here for?'

It seemed the mouth's slit had been a smile. 'Only to see how you're doing. You've walked a fair distance. I've brought you milk and apples.'

'We don't need them.'

'You will.' A bag was dropped on to the tangle of rugs. 'You should feed the baby the milk. Lest it grow sickly.'

As if in agreement, Found began to cry.

'I don't like to hear that. A baby should be happy. It shouldn't be left to grizzle.'

'She's not being left. She's scared. You frightened us.'

'She does a lot of screaming, too.' Leaving Ren no time to ask how she knew this, she demanded, 'What do you do to her?'

Indignant, Ren defended, 'We don't do anything. She has to exercise her lungs. Lil says all babies do it.'

'They may where you come from. What do they care about babies? Whip them, shove them up chimneys, push them down the mines.'

'I don't know what you're talking about. Nobody does that.'

'They do as bad. What's the difference between them things and casting them out to fend for themselves on the streets, or handing them into an SCU?' She heard Ren's breath jump and hiss away drily. 'Well, I suppose that's better than dumping them, small as they come, by the road,' she conceded with an impatient sympathy. 'Let's have a look at this one, see if she's as blooming as you make out.'

Ren gripped the child closer.

The woman's voice rose. 'Let's see. Where's your manners? Didn't your mother teach you respect?'

So, obedient, Ren pushed herself forward, held Found up to the visitor's scrutiny and did not contradict the pronouncement: 'She could do with a bath.' Much later, Ren wished she had been able to make the obvious rejoinder. She was amazed how people did not notice their own smell.

'You'd like a bath, wouldn't you?' the woman addressed Found and put out a hand. Stiff fingers tapped against the child's cheek. Found halted her noise and stared. 'There you are,' the other crowed at her success.

'She'll start again soon,' Ren told her, cross.

'I found young Brocket. Has he told you?'

'No.' She would think about that later. At present she felt uncomfortable about the woman's hand crooked at the baby's back.

'Annie was there at the time, but I saw him first.'

'You know Mrs Gimmer?'

'We travelled together as girls. She wouldn't let me have him. She said I'd taken to wandering too far.'

She leant over the child. Shadows of the hawthorn's branches raked backwards and forwards across her face; they left small flues of darkness in her eyes, her nostrils, behind the points of teeth. 'The poor foundling,' she said as the child resumed her fretful whines and rubbed her knuckles against her mouth.

'We call her Found.'

The other appeared not to hear her. She was absorbed in the child. 'She needs a proper mother to see to her. Why don't you let her sleep? You put her down and cover her up.'

The voice was gentle. Ren heard neither deceit nor threat. So in compliance with the order, she knelt and laid Found on a sleeping-bag in the sparkling light. She said, 'When she cries, Lil knows what to do. She's gone up the fell, but she'll be back soon.'

'That's right. I'd forgot,' the woman murmured.

For a sliver of time there was silence. The shippon was still. On its floor, the dust of peat and bracken remained undisturbed; no noise troubled the stalls; the wind ceased to riffle the hawthorn's branches. Found lay in a nest of rugs, warm and secure.

Then the woman swivelled her head, checked Ren's position, bent down. Two hands sliced through the web of shadows, broke into the moonlight, scrabbled, and the child was swinging up, up through the band of brightness and into the thick dark. There was a second of incredulous quiet. Then Ren was scrambling over the sleeping-bags, shouting: 'Leave her alone,' and the woman was shouldering her aside, thrusting her into blackness where her knees and hands found scratching roots and the litter of thorns. 'Give her back,' she shouted again, and she was by the woman's side, jostling her, trying to snatch, while the surprise of her retaliation pushed the woman into a stall.

'Keep away,' a voice thundered. Planks cracked, broke apart, and somehow Ren, too, was through them. Splinters tore a hand but in the other was something hard and sharp. Now there was no breath for shouting; lungs fuelled only pants and grunts. In the darkness, between the bruising posts and the lacerating walls, Ren was clutching, tearing at clothes, clawing for flesh. The woman who carried Found, screaming against her breast, was straddling another partition and a foot lashed at Ren's face. But the swing missed its target and Ren had her fists clamped round the ankle, was dragged after it, winched by powerful muscles over more planks and dropped on to stone. Where they fought, Ren tossed as if weightless, thrashing like a hooked fish as she hung on to the foot, her opponent unable to use her hands, hampered by Found. Until, attempting to increase her grip, Ren discovered the hindrance in her palm. Without pausing, she flicked it out, gripped the haft firmly against the heel of her thumb and, piercing first the coarse fabric of trousers, layers of flannel and underpants, she plunged the blade deep into the woman's leg.

She heard the squeal tear through the shippon; it lanced the rafters and scraped along the stone walls; it deafened Found's screams. She heard it long after the foot jerked out of her hand and the boot kicked her chin; and the sound of it still rang in her ears as, stretched across the shippon's threshold, she lost consciousness, her hair stiffening as the dew froze upon the slate flags. But that was after she had seen the woman crawl, raise herself painfully, hoist Found on her shoulder and, diminished and gentled by the moon's twilight, limp slowly away.

Not until she was some distance from the shippon did Lil encounter any difficulties on her search. She moved quickly over the scant grass towards the belt of trees they had passed by that morning. Beyond it, the light flashed. But at the trees she was stopped by a wall of rock and it was not an obstacle she could run towards and leap. Impatient at the delay, she peered for handhold crevices, scabs of lichen and minute pits in the vertical face, and though the moon did not give full illumination, she was thankful for its weak light. Without it, she would not have escaped injury when she reached the top. For she had to stride over bottomless cracks between the huge blocks, on a surface that was slippery, polished with moisture, and where puddles lay in the hollows scooped by millennia of rain. Noticing a filament of silver fringing this water, Lil recognised the coming of frost.

Over this hazard, she saw that the distance from the light was greater than she had thought. She was approaching a valley and her goal was on the other side. Descending a long slope, crossing a railway line and a road, she wondered whether the light was an illusion, a trick of the moon.

Or it could be an hallucination, like Great-great-grandpa told about, Lil said to herself. The sort he got when he was wounded. Sailors have them, too, drifting for days in an open boat. But she was not wounded or suffering from exposure. The light was a fact, undeniably there.

Coming to a wide stream, Lil ran beside it, looking for shallow water, a ford, but within a few minutes she had reached a footbridge, was over it and running, her breath clamorous and chest tight. Climbing hillocks and mounds that reared tall as mountains, she saw as she grew closer that the light appeared higher than before and that within its misty aura it seemed to move.

Was this a signal? And if so, to whom?

Lil resisted the question, otherwise her legs might have stopped without her bidding; they might have turned about and carried her back to the shippon which she had left in Ren's trembling guard. She could not allow that. She had been taught to complete a mission; you did not retreat from your goal.

And suddenly she had reached it. Balancing on rubble that had once been a hearth, she looked over the stump of a chimney and there was the light. It came from a lantern fixed to a high pole and shone out undimmed by the moon. Hanging from straps, it was sufficiently loose to swing in the breeze. No one was occupied in sending signals. No one was poised to attack her. Nor did the spur of land she had traversed afford concealment to anyone waiting in ambush.

Lil stood in the ruins of the cottage and her body sagged with relief. She would have liked to rest but she must wait until she was back in the byre, lying in her quilted bag, cocooned against this cold. She could not remember when she last had a full night's sleep. 'It's not clever to push yourself beyond your strength,' she had been told many times. 'Afterwards there can be penalties. For example, you may be less efficient and take foolish risks.'

Thinking of this warning, she looked along the slopes and to the horizon as far as she could see. Above her the lantern fluttered, and she wondered whether telegraph wires had once been strung across this valley and whether this pole was all that remained. It was certainly tall enough. You would need some muscles to shin up that! she admired. And who did it? What was that point of sticking a lantern on the top of a rotten old post?

She stopped and the night was quiet, waiting for her to understand the question. Then she was shouting the answer: 'It has a point! It's been strung up there on purpose. It's a bait. For me. To lure me away.'

Again she was running, away from the light, racing down the hillside, tripping over tussocks and into stiff clumps of reeds. She paddled through plashes; her boots were sucked into the sponge of peat; her trousers wicked the moisture into bands round her calves; her breath rasped. And while she castigated herself for her foolhardy dash to investigate the light and groaned at the trick that had been played on her, one part of her mind was warning her that this was not the way she had come. The river she had crossed had been too wide to leap and had a defined edge. What she could now see was a stream she could straddle, and its water was little deeper than that which covered the marsh. Lil looked at the land around her and acknowledged that she was lost.

For a time she was taken by panic. She felt her knees buckle; she heard the thud of her heart under her ribs; her mouth was a dried husk. There were no landmarks. All she could see ahead of her were ridges, the hint of a prominence, humps.

She did not know how long she wandered; it could have been measured in minutes but her panic insisted it was hours. Time did not tick at a sedate, even pace; it battered and hammered, its strokes irregular but always coming more fast. She hacked through deep bracken, alarmed that she could not discern what it covered; she slopped through slime, fearful of what congealed horrors might lie under its skin; she found courses which seeped up through the peat and she followed their slim threads only to find that they sank again into the earth. She had no thought to comfort her; she could not encourage herself with memories of similar occasions that she had conquered, for never before had she walked alone with a grim fell at her shoulder, never before had she been lost in such a region, barren and wild. The thoughts she did have were of Ren and Found left in the shippon undefended; and her memories were of her people's teaching which she had failed to carry out. With her legs dragging, and her face growing numb in the night frost, Lil trudged, hopeless, her meandering way lit by the leering moon.

No matter how far she roved, she could not discover her tracks, and when at last she came to a bridge, not the one she had crossed earlier, she shook its flimsy structure to prove that it was not a vision her imagination supplied. Later, the sight of the byre was like a mirage, a destination beyond her reach.

But it remained in her quivering vision, looking smaller than she remembered and vulnerable despite its walls of stone. A flimsy fortress with gaping doorway and a hawthorn flapping through its roof. Running towards it, she heard strange scrapings in her throat, whimpers which became sobs as her boots squeaked on slate flags, as she heard metal tinkle against a doorpost, caught sight of a blade filmed with brown, saw clothes, arms skewed over the threshold, and the bruise patching Ren's face.

Twelve

It was Lil's hands chafing hers that brought Ren back to full consciousness. For a time she had lain without sensation or thoughts but as these had sneaked back, bringing the throbs to her body and the memories of what had occurred, Ren could not move. Grief clamped her muscles. She felt the frost rise through the slate flags; she observed the dew grow into crystals over the grass and saw them shine blue under the moon. She was plucked by shivers and felt them cease, numbed as the cold poked to the bone. Not before her stiff body had been heaved, dragged and placed under blankets and her hands pushed inside the sock mittens, was Ren able to speak.

'I couldn't stop it.'

'You tried,' Lil's voice consoled.

'The stone would have worked if there'd been a witch.'

'Stone? You had my knife. Remember? There's a lot of blood. You must have jabbed him hard.'

'Her.'

There was a pause. 'You mean, a woman?'

'She was tall; and so strong.'

'You're sure it wasn't a man?'

'Her voice.' Until she had started screeching. Then she was like a wild beast.

'Can you remember any more?'

'She said . . . she found Brocket.'

'Brocket? Was he left, too?'

'Mrs Gimmer wouldn't let her have him.'

'So now she's after Found? I've got to find her. No, you can't come,' she stated as Ren tried to rise. 'You've been knocked out and you're as stiff as a corpse. Keep under the blankets. When Brocket gets back, say he's to make a fire. The time's past for trying to hide.'

'Where will you look?'

'Where the footprints go. She's made a mistake, stealing Found on a night there is frost.'

It was some time later that Ren, huddled by Brocket's bright fire, recalled how Lil had pushed herself clumsily to her feet, the floor's litter furring her damp knees and the exhaustion bleaching her face.

'I'll follow her soon as I can,' Brocket had promised. 'First thing is to get you warm. Else you'll take sick.'

'I don't care if I do. Please leave me and go after Lil. She'll need help. We have to get Found back. Please, Brocket.'

But she could not persuade him however much she begged. He had nodded and continued to collect kindling for the fire, splitting planks, climbing the shelf above the stalls, throwing down brittle twigs, pulpy wood and handfuls of mouldy hay.

'I've told you, I'm going. I'll be off soon. I'll catch them, Ren.'

He could not tell her how glad he had been to find her in the shippon. He could not have hobbled his imagination if no one had been left. There had been the scuffed prints in the doorway, the splintered wood in the stalls, and finally the tangled bedding. It had taken him several moments to accept that it did not cover Lil or the baby and, examining the bruise on Ren's face, touching her icy cheeks, he had thought she was dead. He wanted to forget the feel of her cold skin under his touch. Then she had moved, breaking his nightmare, and he had told himself: I must warm her up.

When the fire was burning he tugged her to it, draped her with sleeping-bags and blankets. At last, ready to go, he asked, 'What happened?' Aghast, he listened, and watched her tears licked by the light of the flames.

'It's not your fault,' he told her and knew that was no comfort.

'I shouldn't have laid Found down. Just because she told me to. I should've kept hold of the baby.'

'She'd have still got her. She's bigger than you. It would've needed someone her own size.' He did not add: None of us is that.

'Annie Gimmer hadn't let her.'

Brocket thought: Mrs Gimmer has never been in charge of the baby. Ren's feverish. She must be raving. 'Mrs Gimmer would see to it Found wasn't grabbed,' he soothed.

'Not Found. You.' Now that tears had begun there was no time for words.

'Me? Mrs Gimmer hadn't let her grab *me*? When? Who?'

She shook her head. Her body was lifted, jolted by sobs.

Appalled, he said, 'It don't matter.'

Through great retches she managed: 'She travels. Further than Annie Gimmer.'

Brocket considered. There was a memory. It eluded him, a will o' the wisp. He caught a glint of its passage. It led him to the buttress of a lime kiln long abandoned by farmers. Moss furred its curved stones, primroses dotted its entrance; there was a haze of bluebells somewhere by trees, and Annie Gimmer was saying: 'You stay here; try splicing those ropes I've brought; and don't you make a single sound till I get back.'

Mrs Gimmer had been hiding him! 'I never saw anyone,' he murmured. There had been times when he had been shooed away from the shed or barn or shippon that Annie was using.

'She says she found you. Mrs Gimmer wouldn't let her keep you.'

Once he had sneaked back and, unseen by her, he had peeped in.

The place had held nothing of interest, only a mound of old rugs and sacks out of which came a hoarse cawing and stentorian snores.

'Don't cry any more, Ren,' he pleaded, thinking: I need a weapon. But the blade of his penknife was snicked and too short. (He must filch a replacement next time he raided the service station.) Looking round for a piece of timber or a stick that could be used as a bludgeon, he remembered metal glinting on slate flags. He went out, found it, and his fingers closed over the haft. There was a crust of brown on the blade and he shuddered. But he must not be squeamish. Ren had used it.

Returning, he told her, 'I'm taking Lil's knife,' and dropped it into a pocket. However, before he had whispered a farewell, there were noises: a slithering, the bump of a body lurching against wood, the scrape of feet dragged through the floor's loose mulch. Then there was a fat roll carried in the crook of an arm, a sleeve glistening, and a figure leaning into the light of the fire.

It was a second before they recognised that the person was Lil. Her clothes were sodden; her skirts clung to her legs in drenched swathes; under them, her trousers wrapped sopping bands over her flooded boots. Little remained of her cape except a tattered fragment which collared her neck, and down her body-warmer ran a wide slick of green slime. Her hair was a soaked cap from which dripping strands snaked over her shoulders then were threaded by sharp grains of frost.

But it was her face that had caused Ren and Brocket to imagine that they were looking at a stranger. It was unlike any face either of them had seen. It was as wet as her clothing but not with water; it was polished with sweat, and this did not rinse away the streaks of brown soil but glued them more firmly, nor did it cleanse the blood from the split nose and stop it trailing over the lips and down to the chin. But nothing could have washed away the long weals that curved along her jaw and came together in bruised knots at her throat.

'Lil,' was all Ren could manage.

She turned in Ren's direction and her eyes glided over the other's swollen, blotched face, but it seemed that she did not see it, or anything of the girl who had spoken. She merely responded to the voice and stood, regarding the space it had come from.

'Lil,' Ren repeated.

She flinched, and for a moment strove to understand her surroundings but her eyes remained unfocused and her expression continued a blank.

'Shall I take the baby?' Brocket asked her.

Lil started. She drew the bundle back, gripped it against her shoulder.

'You're wringing wet, Lil. Let Ren have Found and I'll help you to dry.'

They waited as Lil, her face immobile, worried at the sounds until gradually she absorbed their meaning. She looked round, found Ren and knelt at her side. But it was some time before she would relinquish the bundle. She pulled the covers from the child's head, removed the sodden helmet, massaged the cold nape and stroked the damp cheeks. She smoothed the blanket on Ren's lap, laid the child upon it and arranged Ren's arms. Then she remained by Ren's knee.

Brocket asked, 'What happened, Lil?'

She jerked away as his hand tapped her shoulder and swung round, an arm thrown up to protect her face.

'It's me, Lil. Brocket. Tell us.'

Her silence was terrible.

'You are with us now, Lil. Safe.'

The word made a crack in her abstraction. Her cheeks twitched.

'And so is Found. You've brought her back.'

She nodded. Laboriously, her lips worked. 'Yes. Not taken again.'

'We're glad, Lil. Has the woman gone?'

She tilted her head, as if listening to a distant noise. 'Gone, now.' She slid away on her knees, leaving damp tracks over the floor. Passing out of the firelight, she reached the corner and squatted under the tree.

Ren screwed up the edge of a blanket and dried the child's face. It looked back at her, white and frightening in its stillness. 'Is she all right?' she appealed.

Delaying the answer, Brocket said, 'We'll take these things off her first,' and they removed stiff oilskin, a strange chequered shawl and hessian wound in tight strips.

'She hasn't taken any hurt,' he pronounced, stating their relief. 'She's dry under all this.' Clasping a hand, he was pleased that the child resisted; it was another good sign. He put more wood on the fire. 'Better get her warmed up,' and he adjusted the blankets and sleeping-bags into a tent for them both. The baby was crying now, but fitfully.

'She's hungry,' he diagnosed. It seemed to be the main complaint of babies. They could be kidnapped, brought back, messed about with, stuck under blankets next to a smoking fire, and the only thing they could think of was the next meal. 'That's why she's making those whines.'

To Ren, they were moans. 'She's tired out,' she said. 'I'll lie down with her in a minute. What about Lil?'

He wished that Ren had not prompted him. He had been planning to collect more sticks, boil some milk for the baby – there was a full billy-can on the floor. He had even thought of gnawing at an apple, for he had found a heap of them near the milk. He would have devised any excuse not to approach Lil.

Her face terrified him. The glazed eyes looked inwards, were fixed upon something else, some demon or horror that had penetrated the bone and taken up residence. A living, mocking presence inside the skull.

Despite this, Brocket forced himself to go to her, to say: 'You have to get out of those clothes, Lil, otherwise you'll catch a fever.'

She did not answer or raise her head, therefore he knelt down and hesitantly, expecting a repulse, he pulled her feet towards him, untied the saturated laces of her boots and dragged them off. Lil took no part in this; she did not kick, or assist with the fused knots. But when he had torn off what remained of her cape and said, 'Your body-warmer, too,' she swung away from his hands and put her own over the zip.

He was tempted to leave her. His thought said to him: Let her take sick, die if she wants; see if I care. But his feet did not move him away from her and his fingers taught hers to grasp the zip's tag and ease it down. After that, there were jerseys and skirts and the great sucking tug of the trousers. At each garment Brocket had to coax, arrange Lil's hands, guide them, lift. He continued until her arms were bare and her shoulders, tawny in the firelight, showed above a grubby vest.

Only once had he seen anyone naked, when years before he had bathed with Annie Gimmer in a pool below a foaming force, and he had felt neither curious nor shy; but now he suddenly knew that Lil wanted privacy. He turned and fetched a covering. Still silent, she allowed him to drape it over her and did not squirm as, using a nappy, he rubbed at her hair. Then somehow he manoeuvred her to where the others were sleeping, slid her into her bag and laid his on top. Her expression did not alter but he was relieved to see her lids flicker and close.

It was not until he had built up the fire and wrung out the wet clothes that Brocket admitted his weariness. When he had decided to help these girls, he had not imagined he would end up being a nurse. Mopping up. Either tears or fell water. Brocket groaned to himself.

The moon had vanished, but the sky had not yet signalled the new day. He hoped that dawn would somehow be delayed, granting him a few hours' sleep. After this night he could hardly remember the previous day, but he knew that it had begun with Mrs Gimmer. She had told him, 'Those maidens have flitted. Take this lantern and say they're to take themselves through the tunnel.' He had carried out her orders – done more. However, he had seen no sign of their hunter and the false trail he had set had been no use. The man after them was far too clever. Brocket corrected: Not a man; a woman. Who had wanted to keep him! He would ask Mrs Gimmer about it. Because memories were floating in. He saw himself sitting on the road, looking at the tyre marks of the lorry in the grit; and he had remained there – for how long? – until fingers had forced a straw full of milk through his lips and a figure had wavered, vanished, reappeared in his misted sight.

He zipped up his jacket, placed his rucksack as a pillow and lay down. Shuffling his haunches, he felt the prick of a point: Lil's knife. His hand moved to his pocket, then stopped. He would keep the knife. Out of harm's way. Lil was always flourishing it and, as soon as Ren had it, she stabbed a person twice her size in the leg. He had often imagined a companion, but he had not created ones who fought with daggers or went chasing after babies in the middle of the night and took a bath during the autumn's first frost.

Reflecting, talking to himself, Brocket remembered a bruised, sobbing face, a shoulder bare and ridged with bone, as were his. More distant, there was harsh panting, the voices of two women, a spiral of dust, and himself being lifted, stuffed into a pouch of clothing and carried off. Until at last these pictures clouded and Brocket slept.

Thus in the last hours of that night Brocket joined Ren and Found in a sleep that was solid and dreamless. None of them was woken by the other beside them. The strange moans and screeches that came from Lil went unheard.

Thirteen

Throughout the next day Lil neither moved nor opened her eyes and the only sound that came from her was the breathing that sawed in her throat.

'Don't you think we ought to wake her?' Ren asked.

'Mrs Gimmer says there's not many cares sleep doesn't settle.'

'How did she get so wet?'

'There's the river.'

'But that's miles away. We walked by the side of it before coming to the viaduct.'

'Not that one, another, in this valley.'

Long before Ren was awake Brocket had been up to examine the tracks outside the shippon. He had been surprised by their number; they radiated in every direction, but he dared not investigate them. He could not risk leaving the girls alone when the woman might reappear. Already he had made a mistake: he had taken no precautions against her the previous night. Waking with that knowledge, immediately checking that Found was still with them, he had felt the sweat blooming his skin. The negligence was inexcusable; he was thankful to have been granted such luck.

'Do you think she swam across?' Ren could not imagine it.

'Down there, it's not much more than a gill. In places you can ford it. And there are footbridges.'

'I suppose she could've slipped in.' Gently Ren traced a finger down the spine of Lil's torn nose.

That and the drenched clothing were all they discussed. They made no reference to the weals on Lil's throat. Neither invited the other to deduce how they had been caused. They wanted to keep their minds away from frightening speculations; and they chose not to talk about whether the woman might return.

Ren merely nodded when Brocket placed a large stick by a tin and told her: 'While I'm out, bang that if you've need. I'm fetching water. I shan't be long.'

When he fitted planks across the doorway she did not remind him of a can of meat he had once placed to ward off a more ghostly menace.

Gradually, however, as the morning passed and no one appeared, they began to feel safer. Brocket even considered having a nap.

'That didn't fetch a blink,' he admired when the billy-can clanked near Lil's head. 'I could do with a kip like that.'

'You can have a sleep if you like.'

'I'll wait till Found goes off.'

They had laid her on her stomach in a patch he had smoothed clean. A low fence of planks they had built round her protected her from draughts and, propped on a wad of clothing, she was able to stretch her arms and dabble her fingers in the stalky dust. Occasionally Ren went to her and worked her legs.

'What's that for?'

'Lil does it. She's teaching Found to crawl.'

'I hope she masters it soon, then. Instead of us carrying, she can just trot behind.'

'Oh, Brocket!' Ren answered and saw him grin.

After that, more cheerful, they worked together as they had done when gathering stones for his cairn. They collected fuel for the fire, tearing wood out of the stalls and climbing to the loft for dried bracken and hay. They hung Lil's clothes over packs to make sure they dried thoroughly. Agreeing that she might scorch, they dragged her in her sleeping-bag to a cooler place. Ren tackled Found's nappy.

'It's not so tight as when Lil does it,' she criticised.

'It's a neat job,' Brocket approved. 'Changing a nappy is not such a stumbling block when you know how.'

'You can do it next time, then,' Ren told him, and smiled at his alarm.

After that, they fed her, both of them nervous and neither pretending to have a superior skill.

'She's letting the purée run down her chin, Brocket, and she hasn't eaten as much as usual. Look, she turns her head from the spoon.'

'She perhaps wants a change. Or maybe she's taken a chill.'

So they dressed her in extra clothing and placed her nearer the fire. 'Not too close,' Ren warned, 'else she'll get blisters.' So they tested the heat on their own skins and discussed distance.

When it came to a meal for themselves, they enjoyed the novelty of food heated over the embers, but they decided they should open only one tin. Counting them, they had been worried that so few were left. 'I'll have to fetch some, when Lil's woken up,' Brocket said.

'We'll all go.'

'We don't all have to trek back.'

'Where to?'

'The cave.'

She heard his fear. 'If we rationed ourselves, perhaps we could get to that freight depot Lil talks about.'

'It's a good tramp.'

'I'll have to do it one day, if Madge doesn't find me first.'

And then, what about me? he asked himself. Easy to answer that: When I've got rid of this lot, I'll do exactly as I did before.

But he could hardly remember what that was and he had decided he enjoyed the company of Lil and Ren. Although Lil always wanted to rule the roost, she was brave and tough; and Ren had her own kind of courage. He was accustomed to the usual sorts of danger such as potholes and precipices, flash floods, boggarts and ghosts, but danger with these girls had more point. It occurred to him that he was responsible for it. If he had not left Found with Ren, she and Lil would not have been chased.

'You'd reach there faster without the baby. I'll take her over, if you want,' he offered.

'I've made her a promise.' She stroked the baby's soft cap of hair.

'Mrs Gimmer'd help. She'd see that other one didn't get her. Found would be better off brought up on the fells.' Babies soon grow up, he told himself. Then he could show her about – all the best places.

'It's nice where Greta lives. It's not all computers. Perhaps when she's bigger someone might bring Found back to show you.'

Brocket nodded, consoling himself with: The special places will keep.

Absorbed in their thoughts, they were startled by a call at the doorway and before either of them could rise, someone entered the shippon and strode between the stalls.

'Good afternoon,' Hilary greeted them, and for a second they could only gape.

He had arrived so suddenly and once again his appearance so contrasted with their own, that he seemed to have stepped from another world. His clothes retained their polished elegance, his complexion its health, and his eyes were neither bloodshot as theirs were, nor ringed with the dark stains of fatigue.

'I trust I'm not intruding,' he responded to their stares. 'This shippon looked a good place to snatch a rest. But it's lucky you are here, because I can tell you . . .' About to step over Lil's bag, he saw that she lay in it, and was arrested by the marks on her sleeping face.

'We've been in some trouble,' Brocket told him.

Hilary nodded, apparently not curious but, looking at Ren, he permitted a raised eyebrow at her bruise.

'It wasn't them fighting each other.' Brocket thought it was necessary to make that clear.

'I'm pleased to hear it. I was thinking I should keep my distance,' and they all laughed.

'She needs something to put on those wounds,' Hilary said, nodding at Lil and unbuckling his pack. Unlike theirs, it smelt of soap and polish and was divided into compartments, all labelled. 'My filing cabinet,' he observed. 'Later, of course, the notes will be transferred to disc.'

Astonished, they watched him don spectacles and study tags. 'Here we are: emergency medication. Cream for boils, no. Burns, no. Constipation?' He looked round, received no bids and returned to his search. 'Chilblains? No. Diarrhoea, no. Emetics – I inherited all this from my father. – Gnat bites, not in this weather. Impetigo, ugh! Lacerations. This is more like it. Lacerations, lesions and minor wounds. This stuff might be worth smearing on that,' he addressed Ren's chin; 'but it seems more appropriate for those,' he prescribed for Lil's weals.

'But you may want it,' Ren said as he handed the tube to her.

'If I do, I can find something else.'

She nodded. It seemed unlikely that he would lack anything when he possessed such a store.

Brocket asked, 'What did you want to tell us?'

'I've come across a cart. I'm afraid it's not a coup with runners but the usual kind, with wheels. If you're interested, I can tell you where to find it.'

'Thanks. It might be worth a try. We have to move on again soon.'

'Not immediately, I hope. I predict another frost.'

'I wish we could stay where it's warm,' Ren murmured.

'You would be advised to. That baby's looking rather off-colour.'

'I expect she's hungry. She didn't eat all her last feed,' Ren told him and tried to soothe the child's whines.

'It might not be a good idea to take her out.'

Brocket agreed, but: 'We're running short of food. We've hardly any left. Trouble is, we're miles from any I know to lay my hands on.'

'There's some in a valley south-east of here.'

'Where? I've never heard of it.'

'Do you know any of the old lead workings?'

'Yes. Which?' Then Brocket added quickly as Hilary pulled out a map, 'Just give me the landmarks.'

The other chanted them off as a finger climbed effortlessly up the fells, coloured brown on the paper, leaped down the vertical scars of limestone and glided along the blue ribbons of rivers and gills.

Brocket thanked him. 'I don't know of anything nearer. I think we'll have a look for it, lift a few tins.'

'You're welcome to take what you wish.'

They had not understood that it was his own food Hilary had offered them. 'I don't like to take yours.' Brocket would have been happier to steal from a cache owned by someone anonymous.

'There's plenty. The only drawback with the frozen stuff is, if you're hungry, you have to wait till it has thawed.'

'This store has electricity!' Ren exclaimed before Brocket had worked that out.

'I just rig up what I need.'

Brocket thought: Rigging up his own electricity! Mrs Gimmer would have a fit.

'Is it far?' Ren asked.

'Quite a distance, and it will take you longer with the baby.' She was crying, wriggling and swinging her head. He watched as Ren

110

took her up, rocked her and patted her back. 'I tell you what: if it would help, I think I could spare the time to fetch you the cart.' He took out a notebook and examined the entries. 'Yes. I'm a little ahead of schedule. It's west-north-west of here. I could be back with it some time tomorrow. Save you the tramp,' he told Brocket. He rose. 'I must be on my way.'

'It's getting late,' Ren said. 'Why don't you sleep here?'

Hilary hesitated. 'I must say you have made it very cosy.'

At the centre of the chamber, the burning wood crackled, shifted and the flames raced upwards, never still. They shook out tassles of amber, swishing the daylight towards the corners where it thickened into dust. Through the gaping rafters the branches of the hawthorn waved as they had done the previous evening, and beyond them was the segment of moon.

'It's quite a temptation,' he admitted, but it was one he could resist. He heaved his equipment on to his shoulders.

Watching him, Brocket thought: He doesn't want to get too mixed up with us. No wonder!

'Oh, there's something else.' Hilary leant against a wooden pillar, in no hurry now that his going was settled. 'About that woman who was searching for Ren – I've recalled her name: Cob.' He saw them exchange glances. 'I've kept a lookout but, I'm sorry, she's been nowhere near my itinerary.'

'Where was that?'

'West. Were you expecting her?'

Brocket flinched. 'Sort of.'

Hilary said, 'I supposed she could still turn up. Funny name, Cob. It should be Pen, shouldn't it? It's the male swan that's called a cob. And she wasn't anything like a swan either, male or female.'

'I can't say I've seen many. They don't congregate on the fells.'

When Hilary had gone, Ren said, dejected, 'So it wasn't Madge or Greta that was looking for me.'

'One of them, someone, will turn up, Ren,' Brocket encouraged her. 'I'd lay a bet on it if I had the cash.'

'It was that Cob looking for me.' She shivered. 'And it was her took Found. Will she really have gone, Brocket?'

'I can't pretend with you, Ren. We just can't be certain whether she's gone for good or not.' They were admitting the fear both had tried to suppress all day.

'We must take turns to be guard.'

'Won't you be frightened, Ren?'

'Not as much as before. You and Lil are still here.'

'I'll take the first shift. I'm not very sleepy,' he lied.

'Shall we put more wood on?' Ren asked.

'I think we might as well keep the fire in.'

Ren slid into her sleeping-bag. 'I've still got your witch stone, Brocket,' she told him as she felt it settle hard on her chest.

'You can keep it.'

She thanked him. 'I like it so much, but if you've always carried it . . .'

'I have, only now Hilary's given me a compass.'

'I don't always understand what he's saying, but he's nice.'

The shippon was warm and still. Only the creaks of Found's breathing and Lil's snores interrupted its peace. Beyond the ragged firelight, the doorway was invisible; the cow stalls did not exist. Outside, the fell was silent.

Ren's anxieties were lulled by the quiet and the soft flames. Her eyes were closing. Tomorrow Hilary would bring the cart; they would pull Found in it; they would reach a store of food. It would be a change to eat enough. And she did not have to struggle to keep awake now. Brocket was keeping watch.

Fourteen

It was not Found's crying or Brocket's summons to do her shift that roused Ren the following morning, but Lil's voice: 'I've been stretched out twenty-four hours. You should've woke me.'

Still curled in a dream of her mother smiling, showing her a newborn child, Ren could not respond.

'You needed a rest,' she heard Brocket say. 'And it's worked.'

'I've got to get off.'

Ren was aware of the ripple of flames. They gilded the child laid on another's knee and cast nervous, agitated patterns upon a young woman's face. It was not her mother's; it belonged to Lil.

She managed to ask her, 'Does your face hurt?'

The other ignored the question and dipped the corner of a rag into a tin, disturbing its faint plume of steam. 'I wish I could give Found a proper bath. She's in a mess, all foul and runny. I bet she caught something off that woman.'

'Why do you say that?' Brocket asked.

'She was another one that stank. When I've finished, I'm going.'

'We have to wait for Hilary.' They told her about his visit and his offer to fetch the cart. 'He says he'll be back by afternoon.'

'That's not soon enough.'

'Half a day won't make much difference to the food,' he objected.

'Food?'

'We're almost cleaned out. I told you. Hilary's lending us some from his store and we're making for that, soon as he brings the cart.'

'I'm not waiting.'

Irritated, he demanded, 'Why're you set on pushing off so quick?'

'It's none of your business.'

'Well, *thank you*. I didn't bring you that lantern. I didn't show you the paths. I didn't lead you to this shippon. It wasn't me that made sure you had shelter. And I didn't do any of the other things, either.' He halted. He did not like to mention that he had put her to bed. The reminder would embarrass them both.

'And I suppose it wasn't you lit on the baby the first night.' She turned to Ren. 'I was never told that. You said you'd found her in that spinney. I never did think much of the lie.'

Ren blushed. Even if Brocket had not been present, she could not have admitted to Lil that she had wanted to keep him to herself.

The other girl sniggered as if she guessed.

She arranged Found's legs astride her knee, took her hands like reins and trotted her up and down, but it was clear that Found did not enjoy it. Her head swayed and she gave thin, fretful cries.

'Is there anything wrong with her?' Ren asked.

'She's probably cutting a new tooth,' Lil diagnosed and lifted the child up to her shoulder.

'Since Ren didn't let on, who was it told you it was me brought the baby?' Brocket demanded.

'Leave me alone, will you?' She was up, Found clutched in her arms. 'I got her back, didn't I? Whatever that old tramp said, I've cared for her as well as anyone could. Better. Her idea was binding her like a mummy in strips of mucky hessian and running off with her into the bitter frost. It's a wonder she's still here after what she's gone through.'

He did not flinch. 'What has she gone through?'

'I got her back. That's all that matters. I got her back. No one else

114

did. So now it's me to decide. And I'm not hanging about, waiting, and she's coming with me.'

Ren began to climb out of her sleeping-bag. Brocket said, 'You can't just walk off with her. She isn't yours.'

'She isn't yours, either. You passed her on.'

'I'm not saying she's mine.' He was almost shouting. 'I don't own her.' What did he own? Nothing except a few bits of broken equipment.

Lil did not answer. She was pushing Found's hands into mittens.

'It's like she's a lump of meat,' Brocket protested. 'First one person grabs her and rushes off and then another.'

'That won't happen again. You're safe with me now,' Lil spoke to the child. She stroked the newly wiped head against her cheek. There the weals were thick and prominent, their colour a dark puce. At Lil's throat where they met, there was a web of scratches and flaps of torn skin.

Ren said, 'Hilary left this ointment. It says on the label: Apply twice daily.'

Lil refused the tube. She was collecting her outer garments, thrusting an arm through the body-warmer while clinging to Found. 'If you're coming, get packed,' she ordered Ren. 'If you aren't ready soon, I shall start.'

Brocket was dismayed to see Ren's hurried obedience. He asked, 'Are you expecting that woman to come here again?'

She pondered over his question. He thought: I'd get more sense out of Mrs Gimmer's goat. 'Are you?'

Lil turned her eyes towards him and, as two nights before, she did not see him. She was looking at someone else. Eventually her sight found him and she answered, 'I saw her off.'

'So, what's wrong with hanging on here for a bit?'

'Stop going on at me, will you?' One-handed, she was cramming clean nappies into her rucksack, baby food, matches. 'I've had enough of this place. I can't stand it. That great hill.' She pointed where, beyond the walls of the shippon, the fell pitched gradually towards the mountain's escarpment. 'All those rocks!' Her voice was shrill. 'I can't bear it. I feel hemmed in.'

'Hemmed in? On this moor?' Brocket laughed, but he followed her to the doorway. 'Which way shall you go, Lil?'

Her gaze swung across the slopes and up the massive hill and her lips worked. 'Not along there.' Where her eyes pointed, there had been tracks, but he had been unable to translate them, transparent smears in the dissolving frost.

Scratched by her fear, Brocket shivered. 'There's a road at the bottom. I'll fetch the push-chair.' He realised that he spoke to her as if she were ailing.

He joined Ren who was packing their belongings, tossed the remaining tins into a bag, scooped dust on to the fire and stamped on the embers until their glow shrivelled and they collapsed into grey flakes of ash. Then, as a sign for Hilary, he laid a line of twigs on the floor, added bent ones for arrow heads and pointed them towards the road.

Taking a track whose ruts made by farm vehicles had long since filled with pebbles and mud, they strode down the lower slopes of the fell. They had all benefited from the day's rest and they covered the ground quickly. Even so, it was not fast enough for Lil. She would race ahead of them for twenty yards or so, then stop and upbraid them. 'Can't you do better than stroll?'

'We'll show you how we can stroll if you aren't careful, and see if you like it,' Brocket told her.

After that she made do with clicking her fingers and chewing a strap she had rammed between her teeth.

They soon reached the railway line and, a little beyond that, the road. 'Did you cross this, the night before last, by any chance?' Brocket asked, pretending innocence, but it was wasted on Lil.

She simply turned south and hurried on.

The road was in better repair than the others they had travelled, therefore Ren and Brocket found pushing the buggy was less laborious. But they could not catch up with Lil. Despite the weight of the baby, she was almost running. From time to time she would glance over her shoulder and look towards the fell they had just left.

'Do you think she's afraid there might be a patrolman?' Ren asked. She was alarmed that they were ignoring this particular threat. 'We ought not to stay on the road.'

'There's no more cover off it, but I reckon the patrols will be pulling out. They're delicate, run at the first hint of frost. And look, on the top there's been snow.' Streaks of white draped down from the long flat crest of the mountain. 'That'll finish them.'

She had to trust him. 'You ought to tell Lil.'

'More likely she's scared that old Cob woman'll turn up.'

'But she said she's seen Cob off.'

'For how long? When she's rested and tended to the leg she might easy come back.'

'What shall we do? What if she tries to grab Found again?'

'She got the worst of it with Lil, so she'll not take on three.'

'Can't we catch up with Lil so that we'd be nearer to Found if Cob jumped out?'

'Don't be such a werrit, Ren. I'd get there. I've got a good turn of speed. Show you sometime.'

When they had walked a little further, Brocket added, 'Lil didn't say it was Cob she had to get clear of. Remember? It was the *place*.' He shivered. 'I know how she feels. There's plenty in these parts are best left alone.'

At last, as the fell and the mountain grew more distant, Lil's pace slackened. Reaching a bridge, she halted and with her back turned to the land they had passed, she looked across the slopes and contemplated the peak which lay ahead.

When they caught up with her, she greeted them with: 'Do you know a path round that?'

Brocket said, 'Yes; nobody ever tried building a road over it.'

This mountain lay like a sleeping creature, the blunt head massive, its spine groomed with snow.

'But me and Ren don't mind if you want to have a climb and give us a wave.'

Lil tutted. 'So we carry on along this road, then?'

'Not before I've had a bite to eat. I'm sick of this rush. So Ren and me are having breakfast. We've pushed it.'

'Let's go another mile or two,' Lil negotiated, and they trudged on.

They stopped at a copse by the side of the road and shuffled through leaves crisp with frost. Above them branches rattled their last leaves.

'I'll just try Found with a drink,' Lil announced. 'She refused her feed this morning.' She drew the child from the sling and they all examined her. She twisted restlessly and her lips screwed.

'She looks pasty,' Ren said. 'Perhaps it's the travelling.'

'It's a certainty I can think of better seasons for it,' Brocket commented. He dredged through brittle undergrowth, dug out the rotting trunk of a tree to serve as a bench and selected a tin for their meal. 'But it can't be helped. Morning or afternoon, with or without the cart, we have to trek to that store.'

'I'm not bothered about the food,' Lil muttered.

'We've guessed that.' However, Brocket did not question her again and Lil was grateful.

Therefore, when they had eaten and were walking up a track, and that harrowing fell was finally behind her, Lil could speak of the terrible night and describe what had occurred.

Fifteen

'When I left the cowhouse, I didn't know where to look,' she told them. 'There was a mess of footprints in the frost so I thought it would be easy, but it wasn't. The prints went everywhere, some round and round the shippon as if the old woman had circled it, over and over again. Like someone crazed. That was the idea those marks gave me, that she was crazy. And I wasn't far wrong.'

'More likely she couldn't make up her mind to go in,' Brocket suggested. 'When you're old, you're plagued with second thoughts, Mrs Gimmer says.'

'She was crazy, I tell you. She'd set her mind on this baby. Whatever the cost.' For some minutes Lil said no more, her head slanted away from them, concealing her expression.

'I followed one set of tracks a good distance before I understood that they were my own. I'd made them coming back to the shippon only ten minutes before, and they were pointing the wrong way! I was going for anything, without properly examining it. I was acting like an amateur, getting sloppy.'

They were incredulous at this confession. Brocket thought: It's nice to hear her criticising herself for a change; while Ren consoled: 'You were tired out, Lil. You'd been up all night.'

'Not then. It wasn't over.

'I was glad there was a moon. It helped me pull myself together and be more patient, and I saw that the line of one set of prints was uneven, and the mark of the left boot slithered. She was limping, wounded in the left leg. You did a good job there, Ren. So at last I had found the right track.

'I didn't know what start she had on me but I reckoned, lame in one leg and carrying a baby, she wouldn't go fast. I misjudged her. She could move as swiftly as me and she was as nimble as anyone a quarter her age.

'At first the footprints were not difficult to follow. Mainly they went over grass that was short, and if they disappeared into bracken I went through where it was flattened and picked up the marks. She was travelling more or less on the level, keeping to the contours of the hillside because of the injured leg. That was a relief. I'd had enough climbing for one night. I should've liked to think up more to encourage myself but I couldn't. I would've given my back teeth to have been in bed.'

Lil paused. There had been strange unintelligible craters; the prints would lead her towards one, then veer round its lip and her steps would be threatened by hollows that were flooded with darkness. She dared not dwell upon what they might harbour or how deep might be their base. She remembered Brocket had told her that these fells were pitted with holes, chimneys and profound shafts that led into passages under the earth, tunnelled by springs. If she were to trip into one of them, crash headlong down the smooth glittering stack, she could not be saved. She would lie torn and smashed while subterranean waters swirled over her. A solitary corpse.

'What is it, Lil?' she heard Ren ask.

'A memory,' she answered, and stifled the moans. As if in sympathy, the child whined drily. Lil pulled her closer.

She went on: 'At some point the tracks stopped. We had hit water. Not a river or a stream, I wished that we had. They have banks. This was the sort that spreads all over, oozing out of the ground. There were prints at the start, in the mud, then they disappeared and I didn't know which direction to take. My boots were already sodden so it was no shock when the water came over the tops, but it slowed me down and seemed to be sucking me in and I was thinking, what'll happen if I can't get out? I couldn't see far. The moon was still there, but it couldn't show where this water ended, or if it went on and on, or if it got deeper. And the picture of Found kept coming to me, of her being dropped in this mucky stuff – it was the colour of treacle – and lying there and sinking till it rose up her head and swilled over her face and filled her nose and mouth and all that was left of her was bubbles.'

'Oh, Lil! No!'

'Yes. By the time I caught up with that woman, I was about as crazy as her.

'I was still splashing, looking for Found instead of signs of the woman, when I had a slice of luck. It was the only one I had in the whole night. I felt a breeze, the sort that sometimes comes to let you know that the night isn't going on for ever and if you hang on for an hour or two, you might see morning. It caught more than me; it found something else and I saw it stir. It wasn't Found, though. When I reached it, the thing was a length of rag. It had been ripped off a skirt and it was soaked in blood. Two strides away from it, there was grass again and a heap of stones. She had bled on those, too. It came over me that, for the first time in my life, I was the hunter and the person I was after was wounded and burdened with a load. I would've been sorry for anyone in that condition in piercing frost, but I couldn't pity her. I picked up the tracks again and went on.

'We were running underneath that mountain and when we came to low tables of stone the way to go was no problem. All I had to do was follow the line of brown spots. Up to then, I hadn't seen her. It's amazing; the slopes are so barren and from a distance seem to offer no cover. But when you're on them there are dips and spurs which cut off your view. You can be quite close to someone without knowing. And I was.

'I reached a narrow channel. It was dry and the prints went down it, then along by its side as water began to seep up. Soon it was a stream. It curved, and there was a space with bushes and great chunks of leaning rock. I was in it before I saw her and she wasn't more than six paces from me, crouched over the water, scooping it in her palm and dashing it on the injured leg. By her side was a bundle. She hadn't heard me; her moans were too loud. All that was needed was a leap forward, and a grab.

'But I didn't do it. I just stood there, trying to get my breath. I couldn't jump when she had her back turned to me. I couldn't come at her from behind. It was impossible if she wasn't facing front. And her leg was sticking out like a crutch, and she was bathing it, bent over as if praying the water to put it right.

'Then she sensed I was behind her. She swung round, saw me, slid to where Found was lying, put herself between us and snarled like a cornered dog.

'If Found hadn't been at stake, I would've run off. She was wearing a cap and its brim was bent, jutting up sharp as a beak. Under it, her skin was like ashes except for her nose which was purple, rawed by the cold, and in the moonlight there were black empty sockets where the eyes should have been; but it shone on her teeth. They had points like fangs, stropped to spike you and rip you open.

'She growled: "So you've come chasing."

' "I'm here for Found."

' "You're not having her."

' "Give her back."

' "This isn't a game. It was a real lantern I strung up for you, not a will o' the wisp."

'And she scooped down and picked Found up.

'It was too late to go for her. When she was holding the baby. I couldn't risk it, and I said to myself: You've got to find some way to fool her. Only, there was nothing I could think of. She had more cunning than me. She'd already proved that by fetching me away with that light. I tried to recall what I'd been told, the lessons and examples, but there wasn't one that fitted. They were all for the streets, where you go armed – I hadn't the knife – and where you can take up a position, avoid arc lamps, and signal for help. I had no tactics for this. I just stood there and she watched. I couldn't see her eyes, but I knew she took in every muscle that moved.

' "She'll soon be hungry," I told her.

' "Don't you try telling me how to go on. I can give you fifty years. You can't even dress her properly. She needs swaddling bands. I saw to them first thing."

' "We've kept her in clean nappies."

' "Not if it hadn't been for me. You filched them I had, saved over the years in readiness."

'That told me that the old-fashioned nappies had been left by this hag. It must have been her head Ren saw at the roof of the barn. I can't work out why she didn't take Found that night.'

Brocket suggested, 'She was very close to where Mrs Gimmer was resting so she had to be wary. She had to wait till she was further off. She wouldn't want to risk Mrs Gimmer interrupting when she was making a snatch.'

'Mrs Gimmer hadn't let her keep Brocket,' Ren reminded her.

Lil nodded and went on: 'She yelled, "You can go your ways. You've a few tiles loose if you think I'm handing her over. She's not yours. I found her. Up a track top of the valley, not far from the big road. I was bringing her along the old peat way. She would've stayed with me if that young Brocket hadn't interfered. If he hadn't stumbled on the pram. I'd left it with the wee creature tidy and slumbering inside it while I climbed down past the cave to the beck.

I had such a thirst on me with the pram-pushing. I should've gone back the moment I heard him, roaming, but I kept on his heels for a bit, see what he was about." '

'It was her stalking me. Not Yordas,' Brocket exclaimed.

'What?'

'It's no matter.'

Lil continued, 'Then she said, "By the time I'd been to the beck and climbed back, that young Brocket had lit on the pram. And he pinched her. Sheer mischief, it was. He didn't know what to do with such a body. He had to pass her on to you."

' "He didn't pass the baby on to me," I told her. I was stalling, trying to keep her talking while I worked out a plan. "It was Ren he gave her to."

' "Wren! More a young vixen at bay with her cub."

' "You frightened her."

' "Not enough. She stuck me like I was a pig."

'Her teeth mashed like pincers in front of her tongue which was rolling round in her mouth and I was thinking: Ren wounded this ogre and I can't get anywhere near her. But my legs were buckling under me; they had covered miles over punishing ground.

'She'd pushed her leg out as if to show me and I said: "That needs another dressing," and she nodded and began to croon over Found. She said to her: "I'll borrow one of your swaddling bands, flower bud. You'll not grudge me that?" She folded back the waterproof and unwrapped her and I could see Found squeezed tight as in a straitjacket, but she was asleep. She even looked comfortable. The old harridan began to unwind a length of the hessian, talking all the time to Found. I thought: She'll have to put Found aside in order to bind the leg. That'll give me a chance. First, I'll jump at her and give a massive clout to the wound; secondly, while she's rolling in pain I'll sink a rabbit punch on her neck; and thirdly I'll grab Found and race off.'

Lil halted her story.

Ren said to herself: So that's how she rescued Found.

While Brocket, more astute and not underestimating the old woman's toughness, thought: That way, Lil wouldn't have kept the baby for long.

Looking at her, they found it hard to relate this girl to the one that had confronted them earlier, the one who had been strident, wilful, claiming a right to the child. Now her face was intense, shocked; nerves plucked in the cheeks and stitched down the ridges of weals.

Brocket prompted, 'She was unwinding one of the swaddling bands she'd put on Found.'

'To make a bandage for her leg,' Ren added.

'Yes.'

They waited for her to continue. Since she began, they had hardly noticed the track they were on, its cavernous ruts and tripping stones, its harsh, endless ascent before it became more level, a smoother road. But suddenly once again they were aware of it. There were shouts and in the distance behind them they saw a figure pulling a cart. Hilary. There was no time then to coax out the rest of what had happened.

Later in the day Brocket took Ren aside and whispered, 'Lil didn't get Found back the way she had planned. Up to then, she hadn't been in enough water to soak her to the skin.'

'She'd waded through that marsh.'

'It would've needed a really deep gill to drench her like that, or a spout or torrent. It's made me wonder if . . .'

Ren caught his shivers. 'I can't forget the wounds on her face. It's as if they were made by claws.'

Sixteen

It was the marks that Hilary first commented upon. 'I hope you had a good rest,' he addressed Lil after his greeting. 'You needed one, having sustained such wounds.'

His words pierced her abstraction but all she could manage was, 'Yes.'

'How are they feeling?'

'They smart.' She was charmed by his interest.

'Your bruise isn't so hectic,' he remarked to Ren.

She nodded. She and Brocket were examining the cart he had brought. It was small, like a trap, boxed in at the sides and balanced on two wheels.

'This'll be a help,' Brocket approved.

'I found some oil and greased the axle.' Hilary pulled the shafts, demonstrating the smooth movement of the wheels.

'Pity a horse doesn't come with it. You've got some rare pulling muscles!'

'I've always kept in training. One of my father's principles.'

'Does he do research in these valleys?' Ren asked.

'He is dead.'

The tone was matter of fact, but Hilary turned his eyes away and, awkward, none of them could think of anything to say to him. But as they stood, gathered round the cart, suddenly each one wished for someone else to be there with them, not irrevocably absent whatever the excuse. Each longed for warmth and shelter and older shoulders upon which could be hung these ceaseless cares. For a few moments the way they must travel was too long for their hunger, for their tired feet and splitting boots.

Then Brocket said, 'It's getting colder.' His words became delicate feathers of steam. 'We must go on.'

They lifted the buggy into the cart but left Found in the sling, deciding it was wiser not to disturb her until she was next fed. To Ren's offer to carry her, Lil answered surprisingly, 'I could do with a rest. But she'd wake if we swopped her over. It's taken her long enough to go to sleep.'

That was true. The child had grumbled and whined during most of their tramp that morning. But she had not disturbed their listening; her noise had so matched the story Lil told.

'I'm going your way until this road nears the tarn,' Hilary told them. 'I want to have a look. It's interesting.'

'Why's that?' Brocket asked.

So Hilary began a discourse on thawing glaciers as they threw their packs into the cart and each took a shaft.

They made a strange caravan over the moorland: the cart pulled by the two boys, one so smart and polished and the other sooty with smoke, his clothing filthy and shapeless, Ren white and scrawny, with bulbous chin, her trainers gaping, a sleeve of her anorak slit open, streaked with an old woman's blood; Lil, her skirts frayed, the tatters of hems fluttering round her ankles, her face swollen and bruised aubergine out of which her eyes stared as through slits in a mask. And lastly, inside the improvised pouch and swinging to the rhythm of Lil's walking was the child, zipped into quilted suit, snugged by a woollen helmet, who made neither movement nor sound.

Therefore it was not her demands but their fatigue which finally halted them.

'I'm starving,' Brocket panted. The others were pleased that

128

someone else had made the admission, but it was too cold to eat by the road. Around them was coarse grassland where cows had once grazed; they could see no shelter. Hilary scrutinised the ground through his binoculars then handed them round.

'See, in the angle of those two walls, that wire and what looks like chopped-up wood?' he pointed out. 'I think there's something behind them.'

So they left the road and pulled the cart up a track still hard after the night's frost. Reaching a heap of posts and the coils of rusted wire, they discovered behind them, a shelter.

'I'd not have guessed that without the binoculars,' Brocket admired.

Ren asked, 'What is it?'

'An old horse box.'

It stood by the stone wall, out of the full draught of the wind. Its wooden panels were warped; one of the doors had vanished but the roof remained sound. Having only two wheels, it rested at a slight tilt, half sunk into the ground. They crawled in and lay down.

'Hay! Best thing in the bed line,' Brocket murmured, his eyes closed.

Lil said, 'I don't like to be reminded of horses.'

'Why not?' Ren asked.

'Security use them. When they're after you down narrow places where they can't get the vans.'

They were quiet, their thoughts quivering.

So my surmise is correct, Hilary said to himself: Lil's fleeing Security; but Ren knows nothing about how they work; she must be an absconder.

Brocket, meanwhile, distressed by the scenes he imagined, went to unpack the buggy and select food.

'Only three tins left,' he reported.

Lil groaned. 'It's bad, marching on an empty stomach, my Great-great-grandpa always said.'

'You don't have to open a tin yet. I've got some stuff. Sorry. I'd forgotten.' Unfastening his rucksack, Hilary pulled out packages of dun-coloured cloth. Inside were dock leaves, the moist flannel of moss, then oat cakes and chunks of crisp meat.

'Rabbit!' Brocket exclaimed.

They divided the meat between them but left half the oatcakes until later. Hilary declined his share of those. 'I've already had a couple. When the old woman handed them to me, she obliged me to sample them.'

'You've seen her again?' Their eating was arrested. Their faces were turned towards the open end of the box. Their eyes were scanning the limitless moorland, searching for the figure Lil had described.

'Not the one I met before.'

'Who, then?'

'I didn't enquire.'

'Mrs Gimmer,' Brocket decided. 'It's her way with meat.'

'She certainly knew you. When she heard I'd be seeing you again, she asked me to give you that food. I tried to tell her where I'd met you before. Have I got that right?' he asked himself. 'I know I gave her a grid reference, or tried to. Now why was that? In the end, of course, directions had to be reduced to landmarks.'

Lil said, 'You'd be useless as a scout, Hilary.'

'I must have been thinking about something else. I know!' The bewilderment left his face. 'She wasn't looking for you. She was searching for the other one.'

'Who?'

'That other old woman I told you about – Cob.'

Lil swung to Brocket. 'What does that mean?'

'Mrs Gimmer suspects it's Cob after Found. She'll be trying to stop her.'

Lil dropped her head; her eyes were on her fingers picking at her skirt. 'I wish she'd come sooner,' she muttered.

Hilary was saying, 'Do you know, I've begun to wonder whether her name comes from cobnuts, rather than having anything to do with swans.'

He looked round, but no one appeared to share his interest. All he received was stares. 'That derivation seems more appropriate, don't you think?' he appealed to Lil.

'She was a devil.'

Brocket told him quietly, 'It's her that kicked Ren on the chin the night she kidnapped Found. Lil fetched her back.'

Hilary blinked, had difficulty with his breathing, swallowed and finally enunciated, 'Do you mind repeating that?'

So they told him. They explained how they came to be in charge of Found, how the girls had fled, mistakenly assuming their pursuer was a patrolman; they described all the signs there had been of their hunter and Brocket's attempt to put her off their track. They narrated Ren's defence when the woman snatched the baby and that Lil had recovered her. Their account took some time and they had to take sips from the bottle of water to refresh their tongues and occasionally get up to shake the cramp from their limbs. While Hilary listened without interrupting, his expression awed.

And although what had happened frightened them all in the telling, it lifted their spirits in an unexpected way. For it reminded them of what they had accomplished and how they had endured. Squashed upon the sloping floor of the horse box, they recounted their story and Hilary was included. Listening, he became one of them.

'It's odd that I didn't notice anyone prowling around,' he commented and was surprised by their smiles.

He was thinking about the weals framing Lil's cheeks. The story had not explained them. Hilary reflected to himself: They must have been made in a desperate fight, and none of them wants to describe it, so I won't ask.

Later, alone with him, Brocket said, 'I could see you were mystified about Lil's wounds. So are Ren and me.'

Therefore Hilary was pleased that he had been tactful and asked no questions. Instead he took a handful of hay, buffed up his boots and said, 'Well, I supposed I should be moving on.'

'It's time Found was fed. She's gone a long time,' Lil remarked and lifted the baby out of the sling.

'She's had a good sleep,' Ren approved. 'It's a shame to wake her up.' Then, alarmed, 'Is anything the matter?'

Because the child's eyes were looking without focus into the dim light of the horse box and did not turn to regard the faces gathered round. And when she was held above Lil's knees, Found did not respond in her usual manner. She did not stretch down her feet but flopped against Lil's chest. She was entirely without vigour, her whole body limp.

'Is it the tooth?' Ren stroked a cheek, white, no longer firm. Found had not the energy to flinch. 'Why doesn't she cry?'

'Give us one of your deafening yells; it'll do you good, Found,' Brocket urged. He was speaking for them all. Noise would have been a relief to them. The child's silence was unbearable.

They knelt round her, examining her, hoping to catch her attention, trying not to compare her with some inert, voiceless doll.

'Snap your fingers in her face.'

'What for?'

'See if she blinks.'

'What'd that tell us?'

Finally Hilary suggested, 'We could try taking her pulse.' No one made a move so, overcoming qualms, he reached for a hand. It did not respond to his touch; the fingers did not circle his. Tiny, they lay on his palm, spread like soft petals, the nails translucent shells. He took the wrist, held it delicately between finger and thumb. 'It's going like mad,' he informed them, and with his eyes on his watch he counted the blood beats. 'But I've no idea what it should be at her age.'

Lil recalled, 'My mother says babies need plenty of liquid when they're teething. Perhaps she's only thirsty.'

Ren said quickly, 'I'll put some water in her bottle.'

They could not tempt her, although each of them tried, and they were afraid she might choke if they pushed the teat into her mouth. All they could do was shake out a few drops and moisten her lips.

'I think this must be more than trouble with cutting a tooth,' Hilary offered.

Ren suggested, 'Perhaps it's something she caught that night with Cob.'

'But if it's a cold, or a fever, wouldn't she be hot?' Brocket asked.

'You would expect so. Has this come on suddenly?'

Hilary's question made them think back, remember how Found had refused food, how she had vomited a little that morning, how her nappy had stunk and how she had fidgeted and fretted.

Ren asked, 'What about those medicines you've got?'

Immediately there was a bustle, Ren helping Hilary to remove them from his pack, Brocket cleaning a space on the floor, Lil placing the child in the centre of it, ready for them to administer pills, linctus, syrups, powders, swabs, antiseptics, inhalers, all the remedies for the ailments that Hilary read out. Each time he did so, they chorused their decision quickly, impatient to come to the one that fitted Found. Until, reaching zootoxin ('What's that?' 'She hasn't got it.'), their hope was finally quenched. They sat in silence round the still baby, and regarded her, helpless, appalled.

Eventually Hilary apologised, 'You see, my father hadn't expected to provide for a baby.'

Lil said, 'We'll have to take her into a health disadvantaged unit.'

'There aren't any.'

'There are where we came from.'

Despite their anxiety, the significance of her suggestion reached them. To save the child, Lil would risk her own future. Their minds could not admit the pictures of her discovery and cruel capture.

'We can't move her again,' Brocket argued. 'We have to do it the other way round, bring help to her. Mrs Gimmer is wandering about looking for Cob. I'll fetch her.'

'Just a minute.' Hilary stayed Brocket, already fastening his anorak. 'Even if you found her, are we sure she would know what to do?'

'She brought me up.'

'Were you ever as ill as this?'

'I don't know.'

'I think it's an antibiotic or something we need. I have stuff like that in my store. The trouble is,' he cautioned as their faces brightened, 'we mustn't give anything unless we've got the diagnosis right.'

'And how do we do that?' Lil demanded. 'You're just being petty.'

Hurt, he said brusquely, 'Better than killing her off. We could find out, if we had the books.'

'Books!' Brocket exclaimed.

Lil told him, 'My great-great-grandfather had a Bible.'

'Sometimes if there was a story I liked, my mother would take a sound-print,' Ren remembered.

'Well, I'm talking about *books*. I know where there are some. It wouldn't take long to flick through and find what is wrong according to the symptoms, then collect what is needed. But the library is boarded up. I should have to break in.'

'Two of us ought to go. I'll come with you.' I will attempt anything, Ren thought, to bring medicines to Found.

'Burglary is my speciality,' Lil interrupted.

Finally, after Lil had admitted that her wound throbbed in the frost, and Ren that she was too tired to keep up the necessary pace, it was agreed that Brocket should accompany Hilary.

They did not delay going. 'Night's coming on, and there's not a deal of moon,' Brocket pointed out.

'The moor way should be clear, though,' Hilary reasoned. 'It's the route traders and monks took across to the abbey.'

'I know, but it's had a bit of time to grass over.'

They laughed in spite of their worry. They were both relieved to be undertaking something positive and were glad to get away.

Ren watched them run down the track to rejoin the road. I shouldn't be standing here, she rebuked herself; I ought to be taking my turn in nursing the baby.

But she did not want to do that. She dreaded the thought of picking up the slack body, of feeling it motionless against her own, not wriggling and full of life. She shrank from the sensation of the head lolling against her cheek and of looking down into eyes that regarded her without recognition.

The figures of the boys were small now, they were being sucked into the dusk. She wished she were with them. She envied them the adventure ahead. Eight days ago, at home in the living-work unit, she would have been unable to contemplate it. Yet here she was, wishing she could take part in stealing books! Ren sighed, turned to the horse box and climbed in.

Seventeen

Ren did not know how long the boys' venture would take and she was glad that neither she nor Lil wore a watch. Adding up the hours they spent nursing the baby would not have shortened each minute; it would not have made the seconds limp past any faster. And on the morning after the boys had left, Ren did not search for a piece of rock to add to her pebbles. She no longer wished to record the days and she hid the eight pebbles away.

The time passed just as slowly when her shift with Found was over and it was her turn to do the tasks. One was to light a fire.

'Is it safe?' she asked Lil, thinking that Cob might still be a threat. 'It could be seen – the smoke.'

'We need boiled water for Found, so even if there's some patrols about, we have to take the risk.' She seemed to dismiss any danger from Cob.

Therefore, following Lil's instructions, Ren collected dry gorse and bracken, found the missing door of the horse box behind the stone wall, broke its bowed panels with one of the posts, constructed a wigwam of the split pieces, struck a sequence of their precious matches, persuaded a flame, and at last balanced a tin of water upon the precarious hearth. Her eyes red in the smoke and her nostrils and lungs repelled by its sour smell, she guarded the tin diligently. The water boiled without mishap and, soon cool, it was dripped patiently between the child's lips.

Yet even this occupation, which seemed to go on for ever, used up no time at all. Afterwards it was still daylight; the sun was fixed in the same place; the appearance of Found had not altered. So Ren did not notice how efficient she had been with the fire and she did not congratulate herself as she searched for water or say: A week ago the idea of being alone on this moor would have finished me off. All her thoughts were given to the baby; the dread that she might not recover dragged at each hour and it was a relief when twilight entered their shelter, heralding the night. That was welcome now. She could whisper to herself: Hilary and Brocket may be here tomorrow; please don't let Found die before they arrive.

She and Lil did all they could think of. They changed her nappy, wiped her mottled face and kept her warm. Remembering that she carried a small packet of glucose, Lil rummaged through her rucksack, searched through her skirts and turned out every pocket. Tracked down, it was dissolved in water and drops of it were squeezed into Found's mouth.

'It restores energy,' Lil explained and they waited, hopeful.

'It's working!' Ren breathed as a nerve pulsed in the cheek and the tongue poked and licked. 'It's a miracle.' But it was short-lived. It produced no other movement.

Lil said, 'We must be losing our marbles, expecting an instant recovery. We'll keep giving it her and we'll have some, too.'

'It's not energy I'm bothered about. It's food.'

'This is as good.'

'No, it isn't. It won't fill me up. It won't stop me feeling that my stomach is swinging inside me like a shrivelled-up bag.'

'You'll get used to it. We did, when it was dangerous to move.'

'My mother used to say, "Considering your size, Ren, I don't know where you put it all. You could out-eat a horse." Do you know what I'd like this minute?'

'A nosebag of tasty oats?'

'One of the Festive Foil dinners my mother used to order for a treat. The tray was so wide, it wouldn't slide down the chute for the groceries; the delivery man had to knock on the door. With the meat there was a sauce and red jelly as well as the gravy, and two veg instead of just one, and real ice-cream with the sponge.'

'I was told that all you eat in the living-work units is dried beef and powdered potatoes.'

'I've never seen those on the Fax-a-Feast menu. There was tenderised steak. I liked the Caribbean barbecue best. It was to go with the leisure-screen pictures of people on a beach. The meat came off in flakes, all crispy, and then there was the bone to suck and, looking at the pictures, you could feel the sun trying to give you a tan.' She paused. 'What would you like?'

'I'd settle for a hotpot with dumplings.'

'There's a hotpot for the picture scenes called Country Idylls.'

'They'd get no orders if it went with Street People Kitchens!'

Down to their last tin, they rationed themselves to three spoonfuls each meal.

'Help yourself to tomato soup,' Lil invited as they crunched the first bean. 'No need to hurry. The goulash won't spoil.'

'These onions are tasty,' Ren told her and placed another bean on her tongue. 'How are the peas?'

'Scrumptious. I'm saving the meat chunks till last.'

'Don't forget the chocolate bun on the side of your plate.'

'That'll do nicely to fill the last hole.'

'I feel a lot better now,' Ren said, sucking the bean gravy from her fingers, gnawing until the skin was puckered and red.

'There's nothing like a hearty dinner to set you up.'

Afterwards, they excused themselves, exclaiming, 'What a silly game.' But they could not prevent it. By the second day, they were thinking about food almost as much as about the baby.

'We mustn't get ill,' Ren murmured, 'or else . . .' She was kneeling by Found, massaging an unresisting hand between her palms.

'Of course we shan't. We've got water. That's all we need.'

'I'll fetch some more.'

Away from the shelter of the horse box, Ren could not dismiss the cold. Inside, dressed in as many layers as Lil, she kept tolerably warm but out on the moor, her clothes seemed flimsy and insubstantial. They flapped as she walked and the cold sneaked through. There were no trees, no fences or even the barrier of derelict buildings to blunt the wind's edge. The faded sun offered no heat. The frost which powdered the moor's distant crests crisped the bracken in her path and stiffened the dew into transparent seeds. When Ren reached the gill, she found icicles ridging the grass; they hung over the flowing water in a ragged fringe. Holding the bottle under and feeling the water's ice grip her fingers she thought: I never knew it could be as cold as this. It never seemed like this on the leisure screen when they showed skiing. At least in the horse box we can keep Found warm.

She must return to her. Dizzy, anxious, she stumbled away from the stream and regained the bare open track.

But it was not empty. There was something ahead of her. It grew larger. Too wretched about the baby to protect herself, Ren shouted, 'Please help.' She heard herself repeating the appeal as the person came closer, leant over her, placed one mittened hand on her arm and another under her chin, raised her face and ordered: 'Stop that! Else you'll get a smack.' Then she was pulled into the matted and smelly wool of a coat and her head was held against Annie Gimmer's chest.

'You're an oddity. I never felt such bones,' she said gently as she released Ren. 'Not looking too good, either. What's all this about?'

'The baby's very ill. We don't know how to get her better.' Gabbling, crying, she explained. Then, 'Will you come?'

'I'll take a look.'

'Hilary met you, didn't he?'

140

'That's right.'

'Did you know the other one, Cob, was after her?'

'I guessed.'

'We think she's probably stopped, now.'

'Yes.'

Had Ren been less urgent and more alert, she might have asked Annie Gimmer how she knew. Instead, she conserved her energy and hurried on.

At the horse box, Annie Gimmer leant against the opening and peered into the shadows. She made no attempt to enter. 'Where is she, then?'

Ren announced, 'I've brought Mrs Gimmer, Lil.'

'Let's have a see at her. Come on!' Annie Gimmer ordered impatiently. 'Hurry up, girl. I'm not after her. I won't lay a finger on her. She's a cursed one, she is, the bother she's brought.'

Ren began to say: 'She can't help that,' but Lil was edging forward. She sat at the end of the horse box, her legs hanging over.

'Show me!'

Obediently Lil turned back the covers, supporting the compliant head.

'That's no cold nor fever nor yet a tooth. How did she come by that, I wonder?'

'She wasn't ill before that old woman Cob snatched her,' Ren argued.

'So she did that, did she? I had hopes she'd give up at the tunnel. Where was that young scoundrel Brocket?'

'He was laying a false trail. He thought—'

'Children's games!' Annie Gimmer interrupted. 'It's about time the lot of you grew up. You can get that baby out of the cold and make her comfy again.'

'What's wrong with her?'

'Something on her insides, I'd say. Some muck she's eaten. And she's dried out.'

'Will she get better?' Ren was not sure that she wanted an answer.

'I'd say it's touch and go.' Reading her expression, Annie Gimmer added, 'It's something we all have to face. It doesn't go away because we don't want it.'

'Can't you do anything?'

'No. It needs medicines.'

'Lil's got some glucose. We're giving her it when we can get it down.'

'That might keep her going for a bit, but it's no cure.'

'I'm not going to let her die,' Ren defied her.

She sighed. 'Well, I must say you've got some spirit.'

Her arm, hooked round her pack, trembled. Ren remembered the sound of her boots shuffling through the track's pebbles; she observed how the skin on her face was pallid, the dirt in the deep wrinkles undisturbed. And suddenly Ren understood that when the old woman had talked about the baby, she had not been unfeeling. She herself was ailing, and old, and she accepted that all life ended.

Desperate, Ren told her, 'Found's not going to die. I love her.'

'Then I hope you have better luck than me.' Her eyes dropped, focused on the girl beside her, and Ren saw that they grieved. She flinched and, blushing, looked away. Ren wished she were older. Then she would have the words that were right for the occasion, be able to ask who was the friend of Annie Gimmer's that had died.

'Don't vex yourself,' she heard the old woman say. Comforting *her*. Annie Gimmer added: 'I'll be going. You're welcome to this; you look like you need something solid inside you. I've no use for it now.' As she swung her pack into the horse box, Lil raised her head and for the first time the other saw her face. Arrested, she observed sympathetically, 'You've been in the wars. Who gave you those slashes?'

She pushed out a hand and, despite Lil's struggles, took hold of her chin and peered at the wounds. She frowned; her back stiffened. There was a sharp ringing silence as she thought, considered, made a deduction. Then she dropped her hand, took in a great snorting draught and began to cackle. Harsh and dry, the sound cracked against their fragile shelter. It came from lips that had done with sympathy; it distorted a face that had put aside sorrow and loss. The cackle was no piteous lamentation. It was a trumpet of delight.

'So you carry Cob's marks!' Annie Gimmer exulted. 'It's fitting, Cob leaving those prints. She had nothing else.' She paused; she became an old woman again, and frail, her brief vigour passed. 'But I've got her here,' she declared bravely, tapping her head. 'Inside.'

Then she demanded, 'And what did you leave on her? Come on! What?'

The colour had left Lil's face. It had drained away so deeply that it seemed no blood was left in the skull. 'I don't know.'

'I found the tracks. There were bandages. You were out by the long cave. She led you a dance, didn't she?'

Lil shrank against the split panels. Her eyes were black with the terror of memory.

Ren gabbled, 'Lil had to go after her. Cob had snatched the baby from me. It was me that did the wounding.'

'Proper little spitfire,' Annie Gimmer mocked. 'I saw the blood. And whose knife drew it? Yours.' She swung back to Lil. 'You carried it here, bringing the ways of the street into these dales. Did you use it to butcher Cob, that night under the moon?'

Butcher. The word sliced through the air, scattering the frost in sharp crystals of blood.

'No!' Ren stammered. She had to force her tongue to move in her dry mouth. 'No! It was left in the barn.'

Annie Gimmer nodded but never for a second did her eyes turn from Lil. 'How did you manage it, without a knife? I know where it happened. I found the lantern. I know where Cob is now. I've seen her cap where it hangs out of reach. Tell me what you did.'

The other's lips worked.

'Tell me, you young demon.'

Lil's body rocked. Her throat rattled.

'Cob kidnapped Found,' Ren repeated. 'She acted like someone mad. It wasn't right to leave Found with her.'

'Who're you to say that? You know less than Cob did about babies; and she wouldn't have dumped her like your folks have the habit of.'

'But Brocket said . . .' She had to continue the argument; she had to protect Lil. 'Brocket said you wanted to stop Cob having her.'

'I did. I tried to catch her but Cob had the advantage of years and was a prime walker. She knew I was after her and she didn't want me telling her to stop the hunting, to go off, take her sulks into the next dale. But hunted or not, this one here had no reason to do what she did.'

To Lil, she shouted, 'And what was that? Tell me. You couldn't have done it fair. It must have been a trick.'

'Lil fights fairly. She didn't attack before Cob saw her. She couldn't do it when Cob's back was turned.' Ren was screaming.

Annie Gimmer was not listening. She repeated, 'You couldn't have done it fair. Cob could tramp over that fell blindfold and not come to grief. It must've been a trick. You'll have been taught plenty of those where you were born. And you'll have been taught as well to seek for revenge. Well, I have not. Revenge is not why I'm walking this moor, though now I've been fetched here, I'm hard put to keep my hands to myself. But I will. And you can tell me how Cob came to be where she is. It's owed her, the knowing. I might settle her drifting ghost if I could tell her I knew. I can't give her bones burial; I can't shroud her broken relics in cotton grass or the sweet leaves of larch. But she might rest decent; she might be appeased if it was known why she lies there. It would be a little comfort in the loneliness if she knew such a memorial was carved in my thoughts.'

Her voice had grown thin; her words were prey for the raw skirring draughts. Lil sat rigid, her expression fixed.

The old woman pushed herself away from the horse box. For a long time she remained, swaying a little; a soft keening rippled her chest. 'It seems we'll have to make shift without, Cob,' she murmured. 'But there's one thing certain. You're not stretched in that deep darkness, a pelt full of smashed bones, because you were careless and missed your step. You never lost your skill.

'And I'm sorry now that I forbade you a say in Brocket's fostering. I kept him to myself, believing a wanderer like you wasn't meet for a nurse. But he might have quietened the longing and your wildness would have passed with the years.'

Ren did not watch her going; her eyes were on Lil. She was making strange noises, not moans but coarse, grating pants as if she had run beyond the power of her muscles and the stretch of her lungs. Not knowing why the thought came to her, Ren said to herself: I wish she would cry.

Aloud, she told her: 'She's gone now, Lil.'

The wrenched breathing did not slacken.

'It's over, Lil. She's not coming back. She won't say those things again.' She searched for other consolation but her mind stopped at a body lying in some profound, black pit. There for ever. Out of reach of burying hands. She could not ask how it came there. The question stuck in her throat. She repeated, 'It's over, Lil.'

Lil raised her head. The skin of her face was taut. Like land under thin snow, the shape of the bones was traced by the low winter light. Still reaching for air, she managed, 'Over?'

Contradicting the word, a shudder commanded her.

'We must get back inside. Found must be kept warm. And we can eat. She's given us food. See,' Ren encouraged, quickly unfastening the straps of Annie's pack. 'She said we could have it. She didn't need it herself.'

Lil looked at the food Ren held out: oat cakes and more meat. Then her shoulders jerked, her head was turned away from the child in her lap as, retching, she vomited. And the watery contents of her stomach fluttered then trailed like thin whey over the frost-silver grass.

Eighteen

When Annie Gimmer left the horse box she followed, for a short distance, the road that the boys had taken. Then she branched off and never returned to it. She was in no hurry to reach her goal and walked slowly. When Hilary and Brocket set out, they were attempting to cover the distance as fast as they could.

'We don't have to keep on this track all the way,' Brocket said.

'I thought it would be easier.'

'It is, but soon there's a short cut.'

However, when they came to the path which curved away from the track, the night was established and the moonlight was fitful as it wove through the clouds.

'It'd be risky with the moon bobbing about,' Brocket judged.

'Then this is the moment to camp down. I didn't noticed this path on the map. You'll have to show me tomorrow.'

'I can find it.'

'I know, but I have to see on the map where I am and where I've been. Else how could I find it again?'

Hilary repeated his request the next morning. 'Is this where we are now?' He tapped his map. 'Past the position marked "water sinks"?'

'That's behind us, just off the road.'

'So we go along this path as far as the gorge. Then what?'

'We cross where it's narrow.'

'But a bridge isn't shown on the map.'

Brocket laughed. 'There wasn't ever much call for one. There's a way down.'

This is what Hilary had feared. He felt sick at the prospect. Trying to find an excuse to avoid the route Brocket proposed, he argued, 'There could be ice.'

That was true, for the frost had struck again in the raw hours before dawn, sliding under the bracken they had laid over their sleeping-bags, needling through the quilted fabric, pricking into clothes until it found the warm skin, and twanging their sleep. 'It might be better to keep to this track,' Hilary said.

'That's further. This way saves time.'

Hilary said no more. He folded up the map, pretending it was a breeze that hindered him from finding the established creases; he handed Brocket a portion of the food he carried, hoping that a joke about iron rations would distract the other from his clumsy, nervous hands. And when they had finished, had rolled up their sleeping-bags and strapped them to their packs, he made sure that he did not delay or lag behind. He even contrived to swing his arms jauntily and to stride out in an eager fashion as they stepped on to the rough, curving moor.

But already his heart was drumming. Before them was a stretch of bare limestone, huge slabs rising out of the grass like enormous setts dropped by a giant hand. Usually Hilary would have paused and examined them and tried to remember all that his father had taught, but today he paid them no attention. He simply concentrated upon getting through them without risking an ankle or bruising a shin. He must have no handicap when he had to descend into this gorge.

It was there on his left, the beginning of it. This great white pavement was coming to an end and, beyond it, was the lip of the facing cliff. Between them must lie the gorge, but he would not look in that direction. He would see it soon enough. And when Brocket turned and brought them to the edge, the gorge was as bad as he had feared. Worse. One glance told him that, making the thumps of his heart grow wilder. He fixed his eyes on the opposite side.

'It's pretty steep,' he remarked, trying to sound careless about a gradient that looked vertical, and he hoped that Brocket would assume the exertion of walking caused his erratic breaths. 'We'd better find somewhere to fix this.' He fingered the rope he carried.

'No need. All we have to worry about is scree.'

Brocket moved forward and almost immediately only his head and shoulders were visible. Hilary adjusted his pack and followed. There was nothing else he could do.

The first few yards were unremarkable. The path went down rocks which formed rough, irregular steps and there were shrubs which provided twigs and branches for him to hold. The boulders he came to were also a help. Great wedges of tumbled rock, they were often his height and he could drag his hands along them, lean into their stable bulk as he circled them. But rounding one, he found nothing. He was standing in the air. His boots might be resting on a path (a path you did not wish to see the angle of, yet all the same, a path) but he, Hilary, was hanging there unsupported. His stomach whirled.

A voice addressed him. It was close but faceless. 'Watch out at that corner, Hilary.'

He heard himself answer: 'What . . . I do?'

'Hold on to the tree and swing on it where the rock juts out.'

The condition of his stomach was affecting other parts of his body; his hands would not grasp the slim bole of the tree; he had to force them to be still before he could latch them round. With his head in some rarefied altitude, it was difficult for him to take breath. Sliding round the tree, using it as a tether, he saw himself losing his grip and shooting out as from a catapult, describing a screaming arc then dropping down, the minutes endless before the final crash. To

149

reach the rock, he had to release his grasp of the tree, plunge, and in that second of time before the rock hit his groin, his skin spouted sweat. He heard, 'Take it slowly! And mind the scree.'

Hilary could not see it. On his right, the cliff face rose up, a mass without limit; on his left, the ground dropped away. He was on a natural shelf running diagonally downwards. It was no wider than the soles of his boots. Any moment now, he thought, I'll black out. The rock at his side was beginning to pulse as if preparing to attack him and butt him off this impossible ledge, but his hands groped, found crevices and narrow facets of stone which provided holds for his fingers. Thus he shuffled sideways, his back turned to the void. Then under him the surface moved. Some of it skittered and rattled. At the same time his fingerholds ended. The opposite cliff was very close, erect, massive; he could see a spout of foam.

'It's lucky there's been no rain; this waterfall's thin as spit,' Brocket shouted up.

Hilary nodded. Between them were the massed scales of the scree.

He had to behave as if this gave no difficulty, as if there were nothing at all alarming about descending an almost perpendicular cliff upon a surface that shifts immediately you put down a foot, and which continues to slip, loose and mobile, so that you feel as if you are raking over some monster's brittle, discarded skin.

'That was clever,' Brocket greeted. 'I allus come down on my bum.'

Hilary did not hear the other's congratulation. His head was tolling with the place where they stood.

Behind him was a fall of water and he was in a narrow trough where the sides of the gorge almost met. High above him the rock rose straight up and, despite the patch of sky, the place was enclosed, dark and threatening. Hilary put his hands on a boulder in front of him and tried to recall his father's explanation of such

150

places, but all he knew was the weakness in his legs and the pain in his stomach which had begun to pitch again.

'Nearly there,' Brocket told him.

Hilary understood then that they had not yet reached the bed of the chasm. He saw a heap of boulders; another fall of water.

'You go down alongside this spout. It's no more slippery than usual,' Brocket said.

Hilary looked at the rocks, at the water as it dropped to its final floor and although that was only fifteen or twenty feet down, he could not move forward. 'I think I'll climb back.'

'You dropped something?'

'No.'

'What, then?'

'I won't be long. I'll find another way.'

'What're you talking about?'

'I'll meet you on the other side.'

'You can't do that. You'll be hours. What's wrong with this?'

'I'm telling you, I can't go down there.'

'Be careful, and you'll get away without wetting your boots!'

'It isn't the water. It's the height.' He had said it and he heard the echo of his voice, shrill and childish, against the frowning rocks.

'But this is nothing! Look where you've come.'

'I daren't.' He wished he had fallen, had plummeted into this pit. He wished he now lay shattered upon the great spikes of rock, his blood trailing over these boulders to foam brown in the fall of this stream.

'It's easy to lose your nerve,' Brocket told him. 'Turn round, crouch down, and grip that bit sticking out, then bring your legs back. I'll guide your feet and tell you when to drop your weight. You can keep your eyes closed, if you like.'

After that, Hilary could not argue. He had to carry on. Like a child he lay upon the topmost boulder, let his feet dangle, and waited until Brocket had caught them and pushed them into a crack. Then he released his clutching fingers and slid downwards while Brocket held on to his waist. He did not notice the water gushing through the fissures that gave him support; he did not feel the scratch of rock on his cheek; and it was much later that he realised the thin bleating he heard had issued from his own mouth. All he was aware of was the weight of his stomach, the clanging in his head, and his unwieldly body that appeared to have been filleted of its bone and muscle and reduced to a limp bag. Until the hands that supported him were removed and he heard: 'There you are. Made it,' and he found himself standing on pebbles over which the water flowed shallowly and he saw the cliff curving round, its base near his feet. He wanted to thank Brocket but he was choked with relief and the sudden invasion of air.

'When you're ready . . .' Brocket pulled at his socks. 'These things are worse than sieves for holes.'

At last Hilary managed: 'Where next?'

For a time they walked beside the stream; the gorge was behind them, the cliffs growing lower. Then they had reached a lane and as they turned east, Hilary said, 'I'm not so bad climbing *up*.'

Brocket laughed. 'We're lucky, then. There's plenty of that ahead.'

'It's just that, sometimes . . .' He wanted to explain.

'You got down. It's just a matter of use.'

'I hope you're right. It's worse when my imagination begins to work.'

'I'll say.'

'Does yours when you are climbing?'

'No. When I remember things I've been told. Stories. But I can't get away from them. Not like you. So it puzzles me why you tramp these dales when you're taken like that.'

'I have to finish what my father started.' He paused; his face twitched. 'Dad was collecting material for a book on this part of the world.'

And as they covered the next miles, panting over knolls, slithering down the banks of gills, striding along abandoned farm tracks, Hilary told Brocket of his father's travels. He described his study of the great convulsions that had heaved the rocks into mountains and shot out the scalding lava; he explained the sliding and crashing of continents, the suck and flood of oceans and the shift of ice and desert as our planet rocked under the cascading sparks of the stars.

'Your dad must have been a real brainbox,' Brocket commented. 'Fancy passing that lot on!' He was envious of Hilary's knowledge.

'Yes. But I didn't inherit his head for heights.'

Hilary said no more and, glancing at his tense face, Brocket thought: Does he have to prove that he can do it, so as not to disappoint his father who is dead? I wonder what my dad, if I've got one, would think about me.

'Do you believe in ghosts?' he asked, but Hilary looked incredulous and shook his head.

They had reached another river, well east of the gorge. 'Where exactly's your place, then?' Brocket asked.

'The other side of this river. Dad liked old lead mines and he made this one his base when he was researching in this area. He used it to store equipment and food, and he camped in it. But the school, where the books are, comes before that. It's in a village after this church in a field.' He consulted the map. 'Do you know it?'

'I know where the old school is.'

'Good. Would you say the village is another three miles?'

'Thereabouts. But I need a snack.'

'I need more than that.' Hilary shared out the chocolate and the thick, solid biscuit. Neither remarked that there was no food left. 'I don't expect we shall reach my store this evening.'

'We can try.' But Brocket thought: Three miles to the library, then a further trek; Hilary's right; we'll be hard pushed to reach his store today; and if we don't, we shan't only be looking for medicines for Found, but for me. Food.

Then they set off again, able to walk faster than before because the path was by the side of the river and along easy, level ground. Now they were concentrating on their immediate goal.

'That old school's been locked up for years,' Brocket remarked.

'Yes, but Dad told me about the books. I don't suppose it was worth anyone's trouble to clear them out.'

They crossed over a suspension bridge, their feet resounding on the frozen planks, and came to a bend in the river.

'Look at that!'

'Where?'

Brocket pointed.

'You mean that green stuff?' Wedged into the river bank, a fallen branch of alder had netted something in its twigs. Hilary peered. 'I'm not wearing my specs.'

'It's a scarf.'

'Yes?'

'It's new.'

'It doesn't look very new to me.'

'I mean: in the water.'

'What makes you say that?'

'It isn't bashed about enough, is it? Bedraggled. If it'd been there a time it'd have bits of weeds and leaves caught on it. It'd be thicker, be its own little weir, with the water swirling round it.'

Hilary was impressed with the other's faculty for observation. 'I see.'

'But that's not top and bottom of it. It's a certainty that scarf's fresh there. Would you like to know why?'

'Go on.'

Brocket grinned. 'It wasn't there last time I was passing.'

Hilary laughed. 'I invited that!'

Brocket did not move on. 'It's only recently dropped in and been stopped by that branch. Before it could be carried to the next bridge.' He nodded downstream in the direction they were walking.

'What's the matter, Brocket?' Hilary asked, for the other's amusement had vanished; his face was sombre. 'Somebody has lost a scarf, that's all.'

'Who, I wonder. Absconders and such don't use this path. They keep mainly to roads.' He paused. 'I wish it hadn't been this particular spot. Do you know what happened here?' Opposite them for a score or so yards the bank of the river rose into a sharp cliff; a few shrubs and ferns striped the ledges and along the crest were hawthorns and a solitary birch. 'Years ago. After a long, long quarrel between two men. One was the doctor who attended folk in this vale. The other was a blacksmith and a drunk. He lived in the last village we passed and he was a sort of highwayman as well as being a blacksmith. The doctor didn't hide his opinion of him; he told the blacksmith that one day he would hang, and the blacksmith got mad and vowed he would stop the doctor's mouth. So he lay in wait and murdered him one night as he was riding through High Wood, then he buried him on the fell. But he got scared that someone would find the grave so he dug him up and carried him to this scar and threw him into the river. It was dead of night but two people walking along this path heard the slap of the corpse in the water and followed it down till they could hook it out.'

'What happened to the blacksmith?'

'He was hanged from the gibbet. But this was where he slung the body into the river. One black winter's night.'

In the lee of the cliff the dusk was gathering, unchallenged by the low pallid sun.

'It's only a scarf floating on the river,' Hilary protested. 'There's nothing else. Nobody has been pushed in.'

Brocket was silent.

'It must have blown off.'

Brocket gestured towards the cliff top. The graceful branches of the silver birch hung quiet and its delicate wisps of twigs were not stirred by the slightest draught.

Nineteen

For the next half mile they did not speak. Hilary wanted to argue. He wanted to say: It's ridiculous to suggest that two people could be thrown off the same cliff; the statistical probability must be one in millions. However, obeying Brocket's cautions, he kept quiet.

Then Brocket stopped. He asked, his voice low, 'Did you see that? Going across the bridge.'

Hilary peered over the other's shoulder and ahead of them to where the stone arches spanned the river. 'What was it?'

'A combat vehicle.'

'Really?'

'Look, there's another!' Brocket exclaimed. 'Or is it?'

'No. Those are the communications boys. That truck's full of screens. The shield things on the roof are aerials.'

'Here's something else. *That* looks nasty.' The vehicle was larger than the others but having no aerial or guns it appeared undistinguished and less important. That was the first impression an observer might form but it was quickly corrected. It was a steel cube with no markings or external features, without windows and having no discernible doors. Sliding noiselessly across the bridge, it was sleek and sinister in the dying light.

'The vent patrol,' Hilary murmured. 'After street people on the run wanted for questioning.'

'Or absconders.'

They squatted under bushes and the leaves of wild rhubarb.

'You've seen these operations before?' Hilary asked.

Brocket nodded. 'A few. But not generally back end of autumn. There aren't so many people getting out, trying their luck.'

'I wonder how long they'll stay. We can't break into the school until they've gone.'

'We haven't time to wait. There's not much light left and we need it.' Brocket's words were almost inaudible as sirens blared near the bridge.

'I don't see how we can force a way in when all this is going on.'

'We'll have to keep to the back.'

There was a revving of engines, a rush of thudding boots, a rattle of shots and a scatter of distant cries.

'Brocket, it's too dangerous to tackle this burglary now.' Again there was a fusillade of shot, the screech of a klaxon and a brief flare of screams. 'Perhaps the vent patrol will have gone by the morning. If we tried at first light tomorrow, we'd be on the road again nearly as soon as if we burgled the school now.'

Brocket remembered the appearance of the baby. 'It strikes me that we can't afford to lose an hour. How long do you think she's got?'

For a time there was no answer. Agitated by the mechanical noises and the clammer of people, three mallards glided over them, braked, skimmed the river, then lifted again with a clap of feathers. At last Hilary said, 'There's one advantage about that siren: it'll mask the sound of us bashing down doors.'

They forced a way through the bushes, climbed a wall and up a small paddock. 'We've come out just behind it,' Brocket said. 'There it is.'

'It's exactly like Dad's description. And still standing.'

'Not for many years more. See how the tiles are slipping. Soon as that starts, it's a goner. We'll try the windows first.'

Cautiously they thrust through a waste of nettles and overgrown plants, their boots crushing a few wrinkled currants the birds had left. At the end of the building was a door; it was made of oak and studded with iron bosses.

'We could've done without the chains and padlocks,' Brocket grumbled. 'Those boards over the windows'll have to be ripped off.'

'They don't go right to the top. Hang on.' Gripping the edge of a board, kicking shallow dents for his toes into the warped surface, Hilary pulled himself up. His head bobbed, then he slithered down. 'The panes are leaded; we could prise some out; but two hands are needed.'

'You heave me. I'm lighter than you.'

He took Hilary's clasp knife, climbed up his back and on to his shoulders. The panes of glass were only just within reach but he managed to prise open the lead, lift out the tiny lights and pass them down. 'Don't want to be heard dropping this glass,' he murmured. Back on the ground, he asked, 'Like to go first?'

'What about you?'

'Tie one of your ropes to a mullion – watch it isn't cracked – and I'll shin up.'

Suddenly there was the pulse of the siren again and engines erupted. They seemed to bear down upon them, coming straight for the school yard.

'The road's close by, the other side of the school,' Brocket explained.

There was a shriek of brakes, the thud of a door, men's voices.

'Get up!' He was crouched, ready for Hilary's feet on his back.

Swaying on Brocket's shoulders, Hilary found that the light was too poor for speed in tying, and the rope would not straighten. Carried for so long round his neck, it retained the curves of its loops and threatened to clench into knots. However, he succeeded in forcing it over the sill, pulling it round the stone mullion and fastening the end while from the front of the school came barking and the heavy pad of running dogs.

'Up!' He heard Brocket hiss and felt his feet pushed. For a second he was raised higher. He grabbed at the stone, scrambled a knee on to the ledge, scraped it over and, a leg each side of the shallow opening, he was squashed double with barely enough room for the passage of his head. Squinting below him, he could see Brocket. He was standing totally motionless, stretched against the wall.

Then at the corner of the building something moved into the low evening light, paws scuffed the ground, a powerful nose sniffed, found a fresh scent. Following it without any meandering or hesitation, a shape advanced to within two feet of the wall. Groomed by the remnant of light, the hair shone glossy, the ears were pricked, the snout twitched and eyes examined Brocket. But the dog appeared puzzled by the boy's stillness. It was accustomed to the panic of flight, to screams and commotion; it could see no racing legs round which to clamp unlockable jaws. The dog stepped closer and gave a short, testing growl.

Watching, Hilary thought: Ought I to slide back and help Brocket? But if I did, the men might get us both; one of us has to escape them; otherwise the baby will die and the girls starve.

Despite this sensible reasoning, Hilary was ashamed. Peering down from his safe position, he felt a coward.

He heard Brocket say: 'There's a good boy,' and, incredibly to his ears, came a short chuckle. The dog did not remove his eyes from Brocket but his spine dipped slightly and his tail flicked.

'Good boy,' Brocket repeated. 'Home now. Home. Find.'

The dog stood undecided. Barking was heard from the road. Reminded of duty, it tensed to jump. But there was a whistle. The poised head swayed, stretched forward; and the dog gave a hoarse bark into Brocket's face then loped away.

Brocket did not move until the dog was round the corner of the building. 'Now!' he hissed.

Hilary threw down the rope, saw the other grab, pull on it and begin to walk the wall, but before he reached the window, Hilary had squeezed back and was over the sill. Hanging from it, his legs dangling, he could feel nothing but emptiness. Then the floor smacked his boots, throwing him into invisible objects; they slid and crashed, echoing, wood against wood. Immediately the shouting outside was halted, then began again, sharpened by purpose. Boots pounded, dogs yapped. On the ceiling a network of shadows sprang darkly, framing brilliant lozenges of light. These were sucked away as the arc lamps left the windows and poked at the chimneys. Rope flopped at Hilary's feet and Brocket was whispering, 'Now they'll search round the back and see the gap in the panes.'

But the siren shrilled again from the bridge, and the boots and the clink of metal and the raucous barking returned to the road. Not until the vehicle had started up, had roared after easier prey, did Hilary release his clutch on Brocket's arm and Brocket let the breath wheeze from his throat.

Disentangling themselves, they remained for a time crouched on the floor. At last Brocket said, 'That was a near one.'

'Not as near as that dog. It would have finished me off.'

'It reckoned there was no use in starting on me. Not enough meat.'

Then they were laughing, taking in great gulps of breaths, choking, rolling about on the floor and knocking into obstacles.

'These crates are bruising,' Brocket gasped.

'They're desks.'

'Are they, now? Fancy sitting at them!'

It was almost dark but they could make out enough to see that the room held only school furniture. Blundering through it, they found a door and beyond that, stairs. Above these was a chamber with unshuttered windows letting in the last light and the promise of stars. Here their feet slithered. They had found another obstacle. Paper. It covered the floor; it rose in gusts of white leaves as they stumbled through it, then it flapped down again, leaving the smell of mould in their nostrils and the taste of mice in their mouths.

'I suppose I shouldn't have expected anything else,' Hilary said. 'When you've got electronic data access, what worth is a book?'

'Are these them?'

'They were once. Before the vandals – patrolmen, I suppose – got to them. They tried burning them, too, only that's not such an easy task.'

He nodded towards the hearth. In it, soft and feathery, was a heap of ashes. The remains of paper, fringed with scorch where the flames had bitten, clung to the soot lining the chimney; others striped with yellow had drifted among the fire irons, poker and tongs.

Scattered round the fireplace and occasionally forming rough piles, were other objects which Brocket could not identify. He poked one gingerly and his finger recoiled as the rotting things gave way under his touch.

'Those are the covers and spines, after they had torn out the pages. Do you know, Brocket, sometimes I think my dad is well out of it. He would have despaired if he'd seen this.'

'There's a lot of damage.' Brocket tried to sympathise. He knew that Hilary was expressing not only his father's feelings but his own. 'I'll look, see if there's any left like they should be.' He thought: Hilary needs a few minutes to himself; he sounds the same as Mrs Gimmer the day she heard one of her traveller friends was dead.

By then it was night. Darkness covered the room but Brocket was used to it. Hands, fingertips, toes, ears and his sense of smell simply took over from eyes. He felt along the walls, found shelves and cabinets, heard their hollow answer to his questioning tap, continued until he reached a dais, climbed upon it, and discovered niches where his hands stroked surfaces that were polished and hard.

'I think I've turned some up,' he shouted, and was rewarded by Hilary's relief.

However, Hilary could not examine the books that night. He could not use his torch or light a fire. The noise at the bridge still threatened.

The next morning, Brocket's first words were: 'They've gone. Sometime in the dark. Did you hear?' Turning over, he saw that Hilary's sleeping–bag was empty.

'We've struck lucky,' Hilary told him from the dais.

'Not before time.'

'Over here, there are lots of medical books and some are quite up to date. Only, the print is too small to read in this light.'

'It's brightening. Listen to the birds.'

'I hadn't noticed.'

Brocket wondered how that was possible. 'They're warning us to get off.' The sooner we go, the sooner we get to Hilary's food store, he said to himself, kneading his empty stomach. 'It's a nice hearth. We could light a fire and warm up a tin if we had one.'

Hilary shrugged away the fantasy and went on riffling through books.

Brocket dragged himself out of his bag. Where it had lain on the litter was a patchwork of torn pages.

'Did the schoolchildren read all these?' He could not imagine it.

'These aren't the sort of books they had in schools.'

'But it was always a school, built centuries ago. A man left the village and made his fortune in London. Got to be Lord Mayor.'

'Like Dick Whittington?'

'Who's he? Anyway, this one came back and built the bridge, Mrs Gimmer says. And this school for the children.'

'I didn't know that.' For a moment, his attention drawn from his research, Hilary looked up, examined the panelled walls, the huge hearth. 'It's handsome. Plenty of space.'

'I reckon I'd rather be outside.'

Hilary allowed his eyes to travel over the floor. The devastation was clearer and looked more shocking in the growing light. 'These books belonged to a man who made this part into his library after the school was closed.'

'Did he read them all?'

'Perhaps. How should I know?' Hilary was impatient with this repeated question. 'Look, I've just turned up a medical dictionary and identified Found's symptoms. I want to jot down the treatment.' He took out his notebook. 'Shan't be long.'

Brocket walked along the shelves of elegant volumes. He wanted to examine them but felt timorous; they were foreign things and daunting, full of hard words. But at last he took one down. Gently he smoothed his fingers down the gilt edges and the leather spine, tooled then lettered in gold. Opening it, he admired the marbled end-papers, turned the pages and found pictures painted in delicate pastels. They were protected by tissue paper, transparent and frail. Opposite them was a mass of indecipherable print but one of the pictures was of two children walking through a forest. They looked lost but seemed to be following a trail of pebbles which shone under the moon. The girl reminded him of Ren. She would like this, he said to himself and, unmindful of its weight, he managed to wedge the book inside the lining of his anorak and pulled the belt tight.

'Ready?' Hilary shouted.

Dawn had now slid down the fells and established itself in the village. They descended from the library, used desks to climb up to the hole they had made in the window, returned to the river path, and, having made sure that the road was empty of patrolmen, they crossed over William Craven's bridge.

Twenty

Brocket said, 'Now which of the old lead workings is your place in?' His arm made a great swooping arc. 'You've plenty to pick from.'

'I haven't approached it from this direction before.' Hilary consulted his map. 'About four miles by road, but there may be a short cut. Here's the store.' He put a finger on the place.

'I don't have much to do with maps.' By which Brocket meant: nothing. However, under the other's guidance, he soon learnt. 'Right. We'll cut straight across. It's all up and down and both sides of this first gill is steep, but not difficult. We can wade it. This is a gill, isn't it? This blue line? And we're aiming beyond that one, to this one here? *Here?*'

'That's it.'

Carefully, feeling his chest tighten, Brocket scrutinised the map, related the position to the one on the ground. Why, of all places that Hilary's father could have chosen, had he lit upon *this*? 'It's a bit off the way I generally go.' He hoped that his voice did not betray him. 'We could lose time. I'm not sure of the paths.'

Hilary lined up north on the map with the compass needle, found their position, placed the compass on it and read the direction of the store. 'It's east-north-east.'

Brocket looked at the little instrument, trying to distract himself. 'That's clever.'

'It's only magnets.' Hilary did not seem to remember that he had given Brocket a compass he could not set. But Brocket was unable to smile.

'This one has a little light in it. See, it works from the heat of your hand. It'll be useful if we need it on the way back.'

'Not if it's my hands round it.' Already they had turned into icicles. He tucked them into his pockets. 'But we shan't have to move in the dark. If we step on it, we'll be there inside an hour and a half. So we can be away long before dusk.'

'From the store? Heavens! I should hope so.'

'I mean, from these parts. They can be nasty, at night.'

'Nasty? You mean, dangerous?' He was thinking about cliffs, potholes, bogs and sudden chasms; he had not heard Brocket's special apprehension. 'We'll have to carry on, whether it's dark or light.'

'Is she as bad as that?'

'She needs antibiotics. The most she's got is another day.'

After that answer, the tightness in Brocket's chest twisted further, becoming a dense knot.

Following the route they had chosen and guided by the compass, they came close to their goal in the estimated time.

'It's soon on our right,' Hilary directed as they strode down a sunken track. It was rutted by carts that had once carried out the lead. 'I suppose when they were working this seam there would be dozens of men milling about and horses and the sound of pumps and all that. It doesn't seem right, does it, without people and noise?'

Brocket agreed with him. Here men had taken over the hillsides, had dug and tunnelled, had brought up stone, ground it and sieved out the lead; and the spoil heaps, which were now malformed grassy humps, and the drifts of grit which lay by the dressing floors and the rusted wheels and the ruins of bouse stalls were all that was left. It was a dreary, abandoned place. Because of its memories it was more lonely than the vast undisturbed spaces of the echoing fells.

'There it is,' Hilary said. Halfway up the face of a low escarpment was an opening roofed by an arch of hewn rock and filled by a rough barrier of stones. Behind that Brocket knew there would be the portal to a worked seam.

'It's a pity your dad couldn't find somewhere else. There are enough sound buildings about.'

'I told you. He liked the old lead mines.'

I bet he didn't know about It, Brocket said to himself, looking along the track. At the bottom, hidden from view by the spur of cliff, ran the gill. One of Its haunts.

They were climbing up to the entrance over soil that was moist and newly turned, not hardened by the recent frost. It's like a heap left by something digging, digging out what it has buried, Brocket groaned to himself.

'This is odd,' Hilary said. 'I didn't leave it like this. I piled this earth against the stones. Someone's been here.'

His mouth dry, Brocket could not tell him: We are very close. Hundreds of people have seen It. Mrs Gimmer says the miners never walked home alone.

'Not that I have any objection if someone needs shelter.' Hilary was defending this seeming meanness. 'Only, I have to prevent any tampering with the equipment. It can't be the fellow who brings batteries and things. He leaves everything as he found it.'

Still prattling, not seeing the hand that Brocket shot out to grab him, Hilary squeezed through the hole.

Immediately there was a startled murmur and the rattle of pebbles. Brocket tried to shout but achieved only a pathetic croak. His mind chanted: Don't leave me half chewed; finish me off straight and make it quick.

But Hilary was not screaming. No grating of chains or crunching of monstrous jaws came from the mine. The sounds were entirely human. Brocket bent forward and put his face to the gap in the stones.

'It's Raymond,' Hilary told him. 'The chap I've just mentioned.'

So the black menace withdrew and Brocket stepped into the store. Little light penetrated the slim entrance but he could make out Hilary and, finally, bunched at his feet, a heap of sodden clothes.

'I haven't got a word of sense out of him yet.'

There was a weak jerk as his hand touched the jacket, an intake of breath and a moan. The head turned and a face looked up. 'Don't!'

They peered at the drawn mouth and the blanched skin. 'Ray, what the hell has happened?'

The lips tried to smile, abandoned the effort and whispered, 'You sound like your dad.'

'He's got to be got out of those clothes,' Brocket said.

He heard a click and above him an electric lamp bobbed. He was standing in a wide passage. Its sides, cut by picks, were vertical; its ceiling was jagged, supported by pillars and beams; its floor was uneven, a bed for chips of shale and the rust-coloured stone. These were washed shallowly by drips of water which fell rhythmic and sharp. That was how, over a century before, it had been left by the miners. Now it held plastic chests, tins of food, drums of water, a ladder, tools and ropes. To Brocket's amazed eyes, its treasures were infinite: a wash bowl fixed in a tripod, a metal plate on which stood pans, a hammock slung from a beam, a web of cables from which radiated wires to boxes which hummed.

Admiring, he remarked, 'Your father meant business.'

'He was thorough.' Hilary pulled blankets out of a steel trunk.

Promising himself an exhaustive inspection later, Brocket knelt by Raymond. 'He needs a fire.'

'I have one, but I'd rather not switch it on if we can avoid it; it uses so much juice.'

The man muttered, 'Don't you bother. The blankets will suffice. You just lay them on.' He seemed not to have understood their intention to remove his wet clothing and when Hilary tried to peel off his jacket he recoiled. 'I can't be doing with that.'

'You'll grow worse lying in it.'

'It's the handling. I'd not be surprised if that shoulder had gone.'

'We'll be careful.'

'I'm telling you to leave off!' But this attempt at authority was fruitless and he was left grumbling, 'It's two against one.'

'That's right.'

It took them some time to undress him. His body was unwieldy, a clumsy dead weight, and an arm swung and poked at an abnormal angle. As they drew off the jacket, body-warmer and jersey, he cried out. But once that was over, he became easier.

Hilary asked, 'Can you manage something to eat, Ray?'

'I'd give it a try.'

So Hilary switched on the hob, selected packets and mixed the contents into a thick soup while Brocket, bewildered by choice, dithered with tins.

'Yan, tyan, tethera, methera, pimp, sethera, lethera, othera, dothera, deek, yandeek, tyandeek, tetheradeek, metheradeek, bumfit,' he chanted.

'Whatever is that?' Hilary demanded. 'Sounds like a spell.'

'Mrs Gimmer taught me. It's the way shepherds used to count sheep.'

'I'd be grateful if you would teach me.'

'Not before I've had a taste of that soup, I hope.' Its smell was enough to begin Raymond's recovery. 'I'm ready for it.'

'We've been ready for days.'

Even so, they forced themselves not to eat until they had fed him. With the right arm useless and the other weak and quivering, he could not carry the food without spills. Therefore Hilary supported him while Brocket spooned it up, feeling shy at performing such a service for a grown man. As his mouth opened, his tongue licked and throat swallowed, he reminded Brocket of Found. Surely babies don't die; die, just like that? he said to himself. Surely she will hold out till night or early morning tomorrow?

But at last permitted to eat, and shovelling up the food, breathing in its fragrance, heaping it on to his tongue, chewing it rapidly between molars, he began to feel more optimistic. The food slid down his gullet, spread warmth and energy inside his chest, and he assured himself: She'll be fine; and Lil and Ren'll have as good a tuck-in as this.

'After that, I reckon I'll see the night through,' Raymond announced though his smile became a grimace at another shaft of pain.

'The problem is, Ray, we can't stay with you.'

'I don't expect it.'

'We're pushed for time. I'll leave you water and some soup in this thermos flask.' Hilary was brisk, moving on to the next job.

Brocket objected, 'We can't leave him like this.'

'Can you suggest an alternative?'

Lying between them, the man muttered, 'I'll manage. I won't start to worry till I hear myself raving.'

'He's in agony with that arm and he's running a temperature. Just think what it's like, left alone in that state.'

'I believe I can imagine it.' Angry, Hilary blushed. 'I don't need to be prompted. So what do we do? Go on, you tell me. It's him or Found.'

'It doesn't need two of us to take the medicine.' Disappointed, he thought: We set out together; we've shared every minute so far. I wanted us to finish it the same way. And then I should be able to tell: Once I knew a young chap, older than me and with schooling and him and me together we did something important. We fetched medicines for a baby.

170

Hilary was staring at him. 'Very well.' His voice was tight. 'You stay with Raymond.' He thought: If I come to another ravine I shan't have him to help me but at least I'll know that once I conquered one.

'No. I'll take the stuff. I'll be there sooner.' Perhaps, he encouraged himself silently, It won't be lurking; there isn't a full moon.

'You don't know how to give an injection.'

'Do you?'

'I've watched.'

'Don't vex yourselves over me,' Raymond interrupted. 'Soon as I've totted up a few hours of decent sleep, I'll get along.'

'Get along!' Brocket exclaimed. 'You're too weak to *crawl*.'

'You shouldn't talk like that. I got here, didn't I?' Holding in the groans, the man raised himself on his uninjured arm. 'You try covering the miles soaked through and with a gammy shoulder after you've been forced off a scar top by dogs and left for dead in the river. How many would have managed that? You name them.'

'You were forced off the scar?' Brocket echoed. 'Where the blacksmith threw down the doctor?'

'They had me in a circle. I hadn't a chance.'

'They found Brocket later.'

He corrected: 'Only the one.'

'Well, this was the whole pack. I thought I was done for when I reached the scar and they closed in. It was either death by mauling or by crashing on to rocks. The dogs were surprised at the one I chose.' Briefly invigorated by the memory, he chuckled. 'I remember the look on the face of one as I went over – disappointed. They set up a howling and ran about, peering over the edge, but not a one of them tried jumping down. Been bred ferocious, but they haven't lost their natural sense.'

'But the water's low, and there the river bed is nothing but plates and slabs of rock.'

'There was a branch of alder, handy for landing on. When the patrol caught up they decided the only thing left with any life in it was my scarf.'

'We saw it yesterday evening.'

'It's been there a day or two. Like I was, till the chance came to move. I didn't want it known I was hereabouts. It's not in my interests at the moment to be answering questions.'

Hilary raised an eyebrow but did not ask him to explain. Instead: 'It's a wonder you haven't contracted pneumonia. I'll stay with you. You wouldn't be in this state if you hadn't been bringing me supplies.'

'I hadn't any on me. That's not why I'm here. There's nothing you can do, except have a go at strapping me up. Then when I've got rid of the shakes, I can move on and finish what I came for. You see . . .' He paused for a moment. 'You see, I had a message to find an absconder.'

'What?'

'Despite Security being on a mopping-up job, I had to get past. I was in haste. Winter's coming early, and it can finish them off sooner than patrolmen.'

'I didn't know you helped absconders,' Hilary said.

'Now and again. Your father was in on it, naturally.'

'He didn't tell me.'

'He would've done when he thought fit. Me delivering stuff here acts as a handy cover when I'm sent on a search.'

Hilary was trying to absorb this new image of his father. To him, he had been a geologist, a scholar, an organiser, a man physically fearless, aware of little other than his work. 'So Dad helped absconders?'

'Street people as well if they had the need. Your father was independent in more ways than one.' Hilary caught Brocket's eye. They were thinking of Lil. 'Anyway, he reckoned most folks are

172

better off in the provinces further north, not so many rules and regulations. And there's a home waiting for this little one.'

Brocket asked, 'What's this absconder's name?'

'It's a funny one. Had to do with trees. What was it? It couldn't be mountain ash. I mean, who would saddle a creature with that?'

'Mountain ash? You must be thinking of rowan,' Hilary supplied.

'That's it. Rowan. Rowena. Have you come across anyone answering to that?'

'No. Look, Brocket, while I see if there is any antibiotic would you choose some packets and tins? The girls will be starving. And there's soup – I made plenty – which is for them as well. It'll stay warm in that other thermos flask. Now the medicines should be in the fridge,' he advised himself. 'I'd be surprised if Dad hadn't stocked any.'

As Hilary turned away, busy and efficient, Raymond grumbled, 'My memory is playing up; must be this chill. That's not right.'

'What isn't?'

'The name. I hadn't heard it before but it seemed suitable, better than Rowena, for a little girl. I remember thinking: And I've got to look for her! Shy, keeping out of the way, not being conspicuous.'

'It doesn't sound like a tree. Could it be Ren?' He held his breath.

'You've got it! Wren. Knew it had to do with trees. Well, bushes; but, still, I was close. Funny how the mind works, isn't it? You'd expect to remember such a name without setback, and I had in my mind a *bird*, but that made me think of trees, you see, so I was led to—'

He would have continued to ramble on but Brocket was calling, 'Hilary, it's not a Rowena he's looking for. It's Ren.'

His words were loud and excited but the hewn walls sent back an echo that was cracked and dissonant, and Brocket thought: Shouldn't I be glad?

Twenty-one

They got through their exclamations; they listened to Raymond's account of the people who helped absconders, any homeless on the run; they told him their story. They arranged when he should collect Ren and he promised to find someone to foster Found. 'I reckon Greta will take her, along with the little lass,' Raymond said. 'That babe sounds in a bad way. You get those antibiotics to her quick. You can leave off your tending to me.'

Hilary and Brocket did not need this urging. They were already packed and they wasted no time discussing whether or not they should split up. Silently they had agreed to remain together for the return. Thus, they stayed not a moment longer than was necessary.

Yet when Hilary switched off the electric lamp and they stood at the mine's entrance, they saw that there was little daylight left.

'You'll never reach there by morning,' Raymond predicted gloomily.

'We can try. We're going a mile north, then taking the road.'

'You'll do well if you get past the field church by dark. You'll have to fit in a rest. Take him to the cave just off the moor lane, Brocket. It's dry and he'll be in good company.'

'What does he mean?' Hilary demanded.

'Some soldiers rested in it centuries ago.' Brocket remembered what Annie Gimmer had taught him. 'They were galloping through the dales, back to Scotland, after a battle or something.'

'That's right,' Raymond said. 'You help yourself to forty winks in there, Hilary.'

'We aren't having forty winks anywhere.'

'They'd set you up to tackle the Monks' Way. At night the cold on it has a dispiriting edge.'

Exasperated, Hilary told him, 'It couldn't be more dispiriting than you!'

'Talk about fuss,' he said as they climbed down from the entrance. 'Anybody would think I was an infant. Some people are like that, aren't they? Grab any chance to offer advice and cautions.'

'He might have thought he owed it to your father.'

'Interfering!' Hilary snorted. 'Trying to boss us about.'

'You bossed him. He didn't want his clothes taking off.'

'That was for his own good.' Hilary dismissed a freedom for Raymond that he claimed for himself, and Brocket would have smiled but it was dusk and they were walking close to Its favourite gill.

It only roams by the water, Brocket encouraged himself; there's nothing to interest It now in this ruined mine; It won't linger here.

But round him the slopes were in shadow and held black caverns behind the collapsed portals of shafts. Floored with setts and roofed with curving blocks, a low tunnel ran into the hillside; down the spikes of fern at its mouth water dribbled and behind was a swallowing darkness, hiding thick muscular shoulders, a sleek pelt. Under his boots the waste left on the dressing floor cracked like discarded bones and, kicking pebbles into an abandoned tub, he heard them clatter like links of a swung chain.

'Hang on,' Hilary halted him. 'I've picked something up.' He limped through the rubble and propped himself against an iron post. 'Nothing there,' he reported, shaking his boot. 'Must be lodged in the sock,' and he began to peel it off. 'Brocket, I know we're in a hurry but this won't take a minute. Don't look so distraught.'

'I don't like this place.'

'I think it's interesting. Haven't you explored it?'

'Not much.'

A few minutes later, reaching the top of the miniature valley, Hilary observed, 'There's a splendid view of the layout from here.'

'I'm not bothered about views.'

'Look. Behind you.'

'Let's get on.' Brocket had no intention of looking behind.

Because It always followed. It never appeared from the side. It always stalked in the quarry's own shadow, close, out of sight.

And the thought of that did not lessen when they reached the road. However much Brocket hurried, he could not shake it off; the creature continued to pace itself to his steps.

'Would you mind slowing down a bit,' Hilary puffed. 'You must have bellows for lungs.'

'We can't afford to dawdle.'

'There isn't any danger of that. More likely we shall take off. Two deafening explosions and we'll be streaking away, a couple of trails of exhaust and two scorched rucksacks orbiting the earth.'

'Don't waste breath. We have to get as far as we can before dark.'

However, the night was approaching fast now; the remnant of daylight was hooded by clouds. Below them the road was a passage where little light poked through the raftering branches, and hedgerows growing on to the cracked tarmac narrowed the walking space.

'All these trees and vegetation are a pleasant change from the ferns and heathers higher up,' Hilary commented.

The other could not agree. They provided cover for a hunting creature and dulled its noise. Therefore, straining his ears for sounds, he answered Hilary's remarks briefly and, discouraged, Hilary talked no more. Except to calculate: 'At this pace, we'll be on the Monks' Way in a couple of hours.'

It will not hound me along that, Brocket assured himself. It dare not trespass there. Its evil shrinks before the power of those righteous ghosts. Once I have reached the Monks' Way, I am safe. Against his protesting muscles, he quickened his pace.

Hilary stated, 'I must have a rest soon.'

'Not yet.'

We must keep on, he urged himself silently. We can't stop. We must stay ahead of It. We must gain that road's sanctuary. If It guesses our goal, It will close in. And as he permitted that thought, Brocket sensed it was answered. Behind him there was a sound, a low warning bay. 'Can't you walk faster?' he demanded.

'No. This is stupid. We have miles yet.'

'Didn't you hear something?'

'What?'

'Listen. A bark.'

'My ears are bursting with this rush. Would it be patrol dogs? They haven't come back?'

'It's not them.'

'How can you be sure?'

'Not that kind of noise.'

'What then, a fox?'

'It's getting nearer.'

'You have more acute ears than I have.'

Brocket pretended to glance over his shoulder. 'You have a look.'

'Can't see anything. Too dark.'

It was never too dark for It to see you, caught in the hot beams of Its eyes. They pierced into your back and spun you round while your legs were thrashed by the whipping chains. He could hear those now. They were slicing through the hedgerow and grinding over the pebbles of the road.

'You wouldn't see a fox, anyway,' Hilary told him.

The chains swung in great swathes but did not hinder the speed of the creature's pursuit.

'A fox doesn't follow humans. There's no danger of attack,' Hilary objected as Brocket began to run.

'We must reach the Monks' Way.'

'It's dangerous to run, blind.'

It was drawing closer. Panting. Not because It was tired and weakening. Because It was impatient. Eager for the kill. 'Can't you hear it?'

'No.'

'You're making too much noise.'

'Brocket, stop! What are you frightened of?'

'This is where It comes.'

'It?'

'Barguest.' He had named it. That was a mistake. It would think It was being called.

'What's that?'

'A dog.'

'A *dog*?'

'Yes.'

'Brocket, you're not running away from a *dog*?'

'I have to.'

'But . . . yesterday . . . you faced the one on patrol.'

'This is different.'

'It couldn't be more fierce.'

'It's a killer.'

'We can settle it. There are two of us.'

'No matter. It would get me. It's on my scent.'

'So was the other. You weren't afraid of him.'

'This attacks from behind.'

'There's nothing behind us. Brocket, are you running away from a ghost?'

'Worse.'

'Tell me.'

'Must save breath.'

'Stop, Brocket! Look! You'll see there is nothing.'

The shafts of the eyes drill into your head; they blind you to all but the gleaming points of the teeth, the saliva frothing over the gums, the steaming lash of the tongue. Then the forelegs leap and your chest is impaled on the daggers of claws. 'If you look, you're done for.'

'You must look. You must see there is nothing following us. Otherwise, you are truly done for.'

The words came in great sucking pants and were overtaken by others loud in his ears. A paw gripped his arm. Claws scored, ripped the flesh, hooked out muscles and bone while his skull was tossed, pounded and cracked on stone like a snail by a thrush. Then the mouth burrowed, obscenely nuzzling. His brain split and was scattered by gnashing jaws.

'Brocket.' Hilary's voice was anxious; his hand was searching Brocket's face, feeling over the head. Above, through the layers of branches, there was a slim stripe of sky. 'Can you sit up?'

Pebbles pressed through the fabric of his anorak, hurting his elbows. As he raised his shoulders he was deafened by the drumming in his head.

'I didn't mean to bring you down,' Hilary apologised. 'Is anything broken?'

'I don't think so.' Along the surface of the road, the wind skimmed icily but his clothes were damp with sweat. Attempting to rise, he discovered that his legs were conquered by tremors.

'You'll be fine in a moment. Panic over.' And Hilary added carefully, 'I don't particularly enjoy travelling in the dark, either. It makes stretches like this so enclosed.'

'It's only in this part I'm bothered.'

'I see.'

Brocket thought: I shouldn't be lying here talking. It could pounce any minute. But with Hilary kneeling over him, that did not seem so likely. In any case, he argued, Barguest would have to champ his way through Hilary first. Almost amused, he added: It would find him tough.

Hilary asked, 'Are there many of these animals about?'

'Just the one.'

'What's the incidence of its appearance?'

'It's enormous, and black and Its eyes . . .'

'I meant, how often is it spotted?'

'It's been stalking people for years. The miners saw It. They say It was the only thing that could scare that blacksmith.'

'Didn't you say he was a drunkard? That's hardly our problem, is it? Also, if this Barguest has been around so long, he's a great age — centuries old — and too decrepit to do much harm. He would be no match for us, especially when we stared him straight in the face.' He twisted Brocket round. The road was empty and unrattled by noises.

'All the same, I might feel uneasy if I walked this road in the dark by myself. Come on.' Hilary bent down, groped and found Brocket's hand. 'What's this?' he asked, a finger searching the other's palm.

'A scratch.'

'It feels deeper than a scratch.'

'The buckle on one of your boots did it.'

'I haven't had them off.' Then: 'I see. It seems years since you were taking me down that gorge.'

When Brocket was on his feet, Hilary joked, 'Have to keep a check on your pulse.' And not until they were out of the corridor of trees, had passed by dense woods, did Hilary loosen his hold on Brocket's wrist.

They stopped once. Though the Monks' Way was straight and open and permitted reasonably fast striding, they were obliged to rest.

'Guess how long we've been walking.' Hilary looked at his watch.

'I don't want to know, else my legs'll think it's time to give up.'

'Mine already do.'

'They might strengthen after a draught of that soup.'

When they had drunk some, Brocket said, 'It's only another couple of hours distant. Can we do it?'

'We'd get it to her by dawn. These few hours might be crucial.'

'That settles it then.'

Their legs ached; their feet were swollen lumps that at every step were ready to burst out of their boots. Their stomachs pitched and rolled; their minds sagged. Never before had either walked such a distance uninterrupted. Brocket reminded himself: It's no further than Mrs Gimmer could manage and, straightening, he gripped the straps of his pack.

Hilary said, 'It's fortunate that my father stocked a good range of medicines.'

'Let's hope they're in time.'

It was that thought that obsessed them during the last miles. The rest was unimportant. Hilary's fear of heights became a transitory handicap; Barguest slunk away, a creature vanquished if challenged; vent patrols and dogs were forgotten. In their dizzy and misting vision there was one thing only: the white, torpid memory of Found.

As they neared the path that led up to the horse box, they tried to run but that was impossible.

'I could do with a nag,' Brocket said, his breath flaying his throat.

'I'd settle for a chairlift.'

'What's that?'

'Tell you later.'

'We'll scare them stiff, arriving in the dark.'

However, Brocket was wrong. As they came to the heap of stakes behind the horse box, a voice reached them: 'I thought I heard you.'

'We've brought food, medicines.'

'I think they're too late,' Ren said.

Twenty-two

When they climbed into the horse box, Brocket was struck by the smell. It was sour and musty, and after hours in the crisp night air, he thought he would choke. He felt that he was entering a place where no breeze or draught had penetrated; it was as if the horse box was a closed, windowless tomb.

'I think we should have a light,' he heard Hilary say.

A torch clicked and its beam arched over the damp hay, over the packs lolling among their scattered contents, over the push-chair strained with used nappies and the last, empty tins. In a corner of this neglect was a sleeping-bag. Lil lay on it, an arm raised against the light.

'Where is she?'

Lil felt for the zip of the bag, but her former deftness had vanished. Snagging and fumbling, her fingers were old and sick.

Brocket said to himself: Is she weak from starving or is it something else? Aloud, he offered: 'Let me,' and Lil did not refuse him.

Inside the bag, stretched by Lil's side, was Found. The light drew nearer, found the woollen helmet, edged down the clammy forehead and touched the closed, sunken eyes. The lids did not flicker. Neither did the mouth open, bubble out a protesting moan.

'She's been like this for . . . I can't remember.' Ren spoke with difficulty.

'Is she drinking?'

'Not much . . . I don't know. Lil had some glue-something.'

'Glucose?'

'Yes.'

'That would help.' Hilary began to search with his torch. 'Where's that lantern you had?' The one that Annie Gimmer had sent to guide them through the railway tunnel. Dully aware that she should assist, Ren groped among the mess of their baggage. Her movements were jerky and feeble.

Brocket knelt to help her. He wanted to explain: We've been walking all night; we're finished; nobody could've been any quicker. Instead, he said, 'She could still live.'

Turning to him, Ren shook her head and watched a tear drip down his face. Her own was stiff and dry; her crying was done.

When they had lit the candle in the lantern, Hilary opened his rucksack and took out the medicines he had brought. 'Antibiotic,' he explained the slim packet. 'It has to be injected.'

Ren did not move. Lil placed a hand on Found's head. In the quiet glow of the lantern, her eyes were expressionless.

Hilary whispered to Brocket, 'This gives me the creeps. What shall we do?'

'Is there any use now?'

'How can I know? We haven't been all that way, gone through . . .' for a moment he paused, ' . . . all that, to give up without trying. If we don't have a try, we might as well have not bothered.'

'But if she's dead . . . we can't . . . I mean, stick a needle . . . if she is . . .'

'Stop saying that!' Hilary's voice rose querulous with desperation. 'An injection can't do any harm. Whether or not. Anyway, we haven't looked.' He bent down and lifted away Lil's hand. Poking among the child's clothing, he found a wrist. 'I can't detect any pulse,' he reported, 'but my hands are so cold they've lost

186

all feeling. Lil, won't you sit up? Unwrap her a bit so that I can listen at her chest.'

Lil did not stir.

Brocket came forward, squatted by the side of Lil's sleeping-bag and lifted the child on to his lap. Her body was limp and sagged against him. 'Ren!' he pleaded.

'I can't,' she whispered.

Therefore, nervous and uncertain, Hilary and Brocket opened zips and buttons, raised the shirt and vest. Underneath the body was wasted, ridged by the hoops of ribs. Hilary put down his head. 'I can't be sure. There may be a beat but the trouble is, my head's still ringing with that walk so there's a lot of interference.' Clumsily he stuffed the undergarments into the leggings. 'Can you take off that top thing, Brocket? We need to get at an arm.'

By this time Brocket was past objections. Already, lifting Found, nursing her, he had schooled himself not to think of her as a corpse because otherwise he could not have done it. He said to himself: When you are dead you go stiff and she isn't stiff, just a bit floppy like a bag without bones, which is funny when I can feel them all, but she isn't *stiff*. In this way he had overcome his nausea and his head did not spin when, following Hilary's request, he took hold of the sleeves of the coat and the woollen jersey and withdrew an arm.

'Hold it,' Hilary ordered and Brocket supported the stick of arm on his hand.

Hilary opened a packet, pulled out a floss of cotton, moistened it with liquid from a bottle and dabbed it above the thin elbow. The vapour from the spirit rose, scraped their throats and, spreading inside the horse box, it cleansed the fetid air.

'The needle is sterilised.' He broke open another packet, removed a syringe, and thrust the point into a capsule. 'It said this is the dose for her age,' he murmured as he siphoned off half. The measure rose up the plastic cylinder.

'It's ready,' Hilary announced and looked towards Lil, but she did not move. He turned to Ren and saw her fists tight by her sides, her eyes pinched closed. 'Lil?' he prompted again but there was no answer.

Hilary knelt there, the syringe lying in his palm. Brocket, his eyes on it, waiting, saw it begin to quiver. 'You do it,' Hilary begged.

Brocket gasped. 'I don't know how.'

'I'll keep the place steady.'

'I'm holding her. I haven't a free hand.'

'You can give her to me.'

Found seemed to be moving. 'Is she waking up?' Brocket asked before he saw that it was his own hand that was causing the bared arm to shake. 'I can't do it,' he moaned.

'Take it. Please. I'll guide you.'

'I'm exhausted. I can't see straight.'

'The same goes for me.'

Brocket thought: This is worse for him than when he was climbing down the gorge. 'We'd better have a rest. After that, we'll manage.'

'She can't wait.'

Then Ren left her corner. She came like an animal crawling, her head bent. 'Show me,' she croaked and picked up the syringe. 'Put it there.'

Hilary placed the point. 'You push on the plunger when you've got the needle in,' he told her.

The baby was propped against Brocket's chest; her arm was held, helpless in Hilary's grasp; the skin lay ready for the needle's prick.

Ren's face was ashen. The shadows thrown by the lantern renewed the bruises on her chin and prised out a nerve which ticked. This disappeared and the jaw tightened. For a second the fingers round the syringe conquered their quaking, jabbed, were halted by the sensation of the point entering, then a thumb pressed down. The child did not flinch.

'That's fine,' Hilary breathed. 'Keep your thumb there till it's all gone in.'

'You tell.' The words were almost inaudible. Ren was looking beyond Brocket's shoulder. She could not lower her eyes to glimpse what her fingers performed.

'It's finished,' Hilary informed her when all the liquid had descended and vanished into the arm. He eased the syringe away.

The child remained motionless. She must be dead, Brocket decided, because he had told himself that if Found were still alive she would immediately react. 'That proves it,' he said.

Hilary asked, 'Proves what?'

Ren's posture had not altered. She was crouched between them, her hand stretched out but empty now. 'It was no use,' she echoed Brocket's deduction. Her body folded, her arms fluttered and, slithering down, she came to rest, insensible, beside Found's meagre chest.

Brocket could not work out afterwards how he and Hilary had managed, though from the evidence next morning he knew what they had done. When he woke, Ren was asleep in her bag and the baby's head lay beside Lil's. But he did no more than glance at Found; he did not listen for breathing. In the chill dawn he did not wish to risk learning that the antibiotic had not arrived in time. And his stomach was demanding food. 'In my rucksack,' he instructed his legs and levered himself up.

On his feet, he could not straighten and the tilt of the floor seemed steeper than the sides of the gorge. The two yards to the pack were longer than the miles they had walked the previous night and along the route were scattered packets, a half-empty capsule and a discarded syringe. Unmanageable, his groping hands knocked over a lantern in which a bristle of wick was preserved in a solid puddle of wax. And when at last he reached the rucksack his eyes, still misty, did not scrutinise it nor did his dizzy brain puzzle over what it held. The goat's milk with the skin from boiling slid like liquid satin down his throat and the chunks of roasted rabbit rolled fragrant over his tongue. When he returned to his bag, his body was still heavy but stronger and he passed into tranquil sleep.

He would have continued all day had not Hilary roused him. 'It's time for another injection. I suppose you'd better eat first.'

'I already have.'

'So have we.' Although Hilary was pale, the food and rest had restored him and he was brisk, hopeful.

Encouraged, Brocket asked, 'Is the antibiotic working?'

'She's definitely breathing and there seems more life in her than there was in the night.'

That was true also of Ren and Lil. They were sitting at the door of the horse box. Behind them were opened tins scraped clean, and now they were finishing off the soup that had been brought in the flask.

'There hasn't been a squeak from them for ages,' Hilary said. 'Open a can and they go mad.'

Found lay curled in a nest of hay lined with a rag of blanket. It was difficult to determine exactly the change in her, but it was definitely there. Peering at her, Brocket decided that this was something to do with her skin. It looked less spongy.

Watching Hilary prepare the syringe, he asked, 'Who's doing it?'

'Ren says she will.' Hilary lowered his voice. 'Brocket, be warned. I think Lil has gone a bit odd.'

'She looks the same to me.'

'It's her manner. Anyway, Ren has taken this on. She seems quite eager, I expect because the baby is not . . . There's a chance that Found will survive.'

Thus the injection went more smoothly than the first and although her eyes were blinking and her lips were sucked between her teeth, Ren dared to look.

After that, Brocket made a fire and they boiled water Hilary fetched from the gill. 'Dehydration is the real danger – being dried up,' he told them. 'So we have to get liquid into her.'

'That's what Annie Gimmer said.'

Brocket exclaimed, 'Mrs Gimmer's been *here*?'

'Yes.'

'Why?'

Ren murmured, 'She's been searching for Cob.'

Brocket nodded. 'I hope you told her Cob's given up the hunt. Mrs Gimmer's been tramping about for days. When was it, Hilary, you came across her?'

Hilary closed his eyes and tried to recall the occasion. 'I know I told you in here before we discovered Found was ill. So when did I meet her? Of course! It was the same evening I'd found you in the shippon; I was going back for the cart. Perhaps it was a week ago?' He frowned, calculating. 'Good heavens, no! It's less than four days.'

'I'm stumped why she came as far south as this.' Momentarily Brocket admired his knowledge of the compass. 'She's old. Nowadays she doesn't journey further down than the head of the river. What did she say?' he asked Ren.

'There was something she wanted to find out,' Ren stammered, aware of Lil's agitation.

'What was that?'

But he was not answered. Lil moaned, pushed herself from their circle and scrambled towards her bag. There she stretched out, her back turned to them, and an arm over her face.

Brocket's eyes followed her but his mind was on Annie Gimmer. He remembered his breakfast of goat's milk and meat. 'Mrs Gimmer gave you food. I ate it. Why didn't you? You were half-starving.'

'Lil couldn't face it, and I couldn't either. Every time we tried, we remembered what she'd said about Cob.'

Brocket hardly heard her answer. He had recalled something else. 'Mrs Gimmer left her pack.'

'She said she'd no use for it any more.'

'I see.' He got up. 'I must go to her.'

Hilary tried to restrain him. 'You need more rest. You may have to tramp miles.'

'Not many. I know where she'll be. It's no more than an hour away, due south of here.'

'I'll come with you.'

'You can't, Hilary. There's Found.'

'I'll come soon, then. Where to?'

Brocket was already out of the horse box and making for the path. 'A cave under a long scar.' That is where she had said he must lay her.

'How do you know she'll be there?'

'Where else would she go when she'd given away her food and left her pack?' he shouted and began to run.

Ren called after him, 'Don't you want your rucksack?'

But Brocket ignored her. He was listening to Annie's instructions: 'You bury me in that cave.' And her grim joke: 'That is, if I go first.'

'You don't have to stay to help with the next injection,' Ren told Hilary. 'I can manage it. Will you leave me your watch?'

He latched it round her wrist where it slid about loose as a bangle. 'Don't forget the water. Try to get some into her.'

'Yes.'

As he fastened up his jacket and collected his equipment, Hilary told her, 'I must confess I'm totally at sea. What's the mystery? Why?' He nodded towards Lil.

Ren indicated a warning and led him out. 'Annie Gimmer was certain that Cob is dead and she seemed to think it was Lil's fault,' she began.

Despite Ren's precautions, Lil heard her whispers. For a few minutes she lay on her sleeping-bag, her mind clanging with Annie Gimmer's words. However much she concentrated her eyes on the roof or the patch of sky at the door, she could not see them. They were covered with pictures of a torch beam rushing down a rock-toothed passage, of a bundle placed between roots, of a black coat skimming the frost-pearled grass and a gaunt face turned to challenge. With a tearless sob, she rose, knelt by Found, drew a finger down a cheek, then slithered towards Brocket's pack.

Just as she had checked the contents of Ren's rucksack, so she went through this, arguing to herself: It must be here; I've looked everywhere else. Then she sighed, satisfied, as digging right to the bottom, her fingers found the knife. Pulling it out, she weighed it in her palm, tested her grip on the haft and touched the needle point. Silently she rejoiced at possessing a thing so efficient and suited to her purpose. But it bore a blemish. Iridescent in the dim light, a stain ran down the length of the blade. Puzzling, Lil held it closer, then, with an exclamation of disgust, she spat on the hem of a skirt and cleaned away this last remnant of Cob's blood.

Twenty-three

Outside, having set his course, Hilary told Ren, 'I don't expect it'll be long before we're back.'

It was embarrassing, the way she wanted to smile when she should be thinking about their search for Annie Gimmer.

'Sure you'll be able to cope? You may have to deal with the whole lot since Lil is so – how shall I put it? – unpredictable.'

'I'll be fine.' She wanted him to go. She could not restrain the laughing much longer. 'If you hurry you might catch Brocket up.' She wished she could give him a push.

'Not much hope of that. He doesn't have legs. He has pistons.'

And when at last Hilary did leave her, she waited until he had disappeared over a knoll before she let the gladness flow. Listening to what he had told her, she had had to hide the grin and hold her hands tightly behind her to prevent her arms rotating like propellers. But now she could release them and she could let her feet dance and her legs kick and her throat expel the laughter. Although Found's illness was not over and Lil was strange and Brocket was imagining the worst for Annie Gimmer, her fortunes were improving. Her own fortunes, hers, Ren's. Someone was coming for her. The moment that Hilary had said, 'Gracious, Ren, there's something I've forgotten to tell you,' she had known what it was going to be. Therefore she had been able to be patient as he had apologised: 'We were so tired, and busy with Found as soon as we got back, and you passed out, and then this morning I didn't remember because, well, there was so much to do.' But at last he had finally given her the news.

After it, everything was different. The sky was not so lofty; it did not dwarf her. The clouds frothed jollily and did not shut away the sun. The wind did not scrape but tapped on her cheeks. Around her, the land was no longer hostile. White rocks in the distance glittered and winked. Nearer, leaves fell from a tree like fluttering moths. The last hips on a dog rose were plump and polished and the bunches of haws that remained swung like scarlet beads. The wail of a curlew adopted a festive note.

Invigorated, flushed, Ren entered the horse box. 'Lil, guess who Hilary and Brocket have met,' she called.

But Lil's answer was: 'Go away!'

'Lil,' she shouted again, and saw the slim blade of metal poised over a wrist, and she was leaping forward, was down on a struggling body, was fighting for the hand, was sinking her teeth in the knotted fingers and prising out the knife. Immediately the flesh of a palm opened, red spurted and Lil was screaming, 'Give it back!' Fists beat at her chest, feet kicked her legs. Then she was standing under the sky where blood, strangely warm, spotted her face as she raised her arm, turned it round and round like a wheel and sent the dripping knife from her hand to curve up, then drop into bracken, to be buried at the roots.

'Curse you,' Lil yelled behind her. She jumped down from the horse box, her eyes on the path the knife had taken.

'Leave it,' Ren ordered and made a grab.

Lil flung her hand away, saw the blood flirt and its print on her sleeve. 'You're cut,' she exclaimed in wonder. 'It wasn't you it was meant for.' Then she was rolling on the grass and was howling: 'It's you that's cut and it should be me. I didn't mean that to happen to you. You're the last person I'd want to do harm to, Ren. I'm telling you, Ren. Truly. That cut wasn't meant for you.'

'You didn't do it. It was me dragging the knife away. I don't expect it's very deep.' Contradicting her, the blood continued to run; it formed a soft cone at the base of her thumb and dropped on to her boot. Ren wondered how long it would be before she had none left.

Lil was curled on the ground; her clothes were patched with damp. Her howling had subsided but Ren suspected her silence. It was possible that Lil was waiting her chance to spring up and search for the knife.

'I can't bandage this by myself, not with one hand.' She was pleased with this cunning. Stretching down, she said, 'Come on, you'll have to help me.' Lil nodded and together they returned to the horse box.

'It needs washing,' Lil said mechanically.

'What with?'

'A nappy would have done, but . . .'

They were all soiled; they covered the seat of the buggy in damp, slimy hanks. 'What a stink!' Lil's nostrils were twitching. 'The whole place is a mess.'

'I hadn't noticed.'

'It's worse than that cave I found you in. It'll have to be cleaned out.'

Lil did this after they had torn a shirt into strips and bandaged Ren's palm. She scrambled about, gathered up litter, washed out tins, shook the sleeping-bags, while Ren fetched more wood for the fire. Lil explained, 'The clothes need an airing and we can hang them near it.' To do that, she made coat stands with stakes that she drove into the ground.

'I like that.' Ren felt that, despite her energy, Lil still needed encouragement. 'It's nice to have a fire without risks,' she chatted. 'Hilary and Brocket saw a big mopping-up. That means the patrolmen have really gone, till the spring. You don't look very pleased, Lil.'

Lil nodded but her vigour had passed.

Ren decided that this was not the moment to tell her about Raymond. 'What's the matter, Lil?'

The other's eyes were on the fabric binding her hand. There was a soggy patch in the centre where the blood had seeped through. 'It doesn't hurt,' Ren assured her, thinking: Any minute now, she'll be out searching for that knife. She slid over to Found. 'I reckon that antibiotic is working. Look!'

But Lil did not stir. 'Brocket's gone after Mrs Gimmer, hasn't he? So it'll all come out. But I had to get Found back, didn't I?'

'Yes, and you did.'

'I'd been drilled, you see, but I'd never done it.'

'Done it?'

'I hadn't been taught out on a fell where you don't know what's under your feet. They hadn't thought of that. They should've trained us for it, shouldn't they? I mean, is it fair? Am I to blame?'

'Nobody says you are. Cob stole Found.'

'What's stealing? I've stole. We all do.'

'Not babies.'

'But it's better to steal them, to steal because you mean to look after them, than to throw them out. Yet nobody who dumps them gets what Cob got. It wasn't deserved. She was ugly and old and stinking and savage as a wild beast but she didn't deserve what she got. Nobody ever mentioned that. It was simple. If anyone puts up a fight, they used to say, he is the enemy. Don't think. Act.'

'They knew best, Lil,' she tried to placate. Astonished, she thought: I'm saying that to a street person! I'm saying her people should live like that!

Lil looked at her. 'You've been brought up to believe the grown-ups know best. We both have. They say: Listen to us and you'll learn. But there are things they don't teach. Perhaps they can't. Perhaps they don't know how.'

'Lil, let's not talk for a bit.' She no longer wanted to hear the details of the fight with Cob. 'It's over. You did what you had to. Nobody taught me anything like that.'

'There wasn't the need. You lived behind squads of guards.'

'They weren't any help when I was brought here. What would've happened to me if you hadn't come?'

For a moment Lil smiled. 'You'd have got by.' Then she said, 'I got plenty of training, Ren, but it missed something out. I did what they taught me, but they hadn't told me how it would *feel*.'

It was twilight and Ren was stoking up the fire when the boys returned.

Hilary's greeting was: 'How is she? You managed the next injection? Is she taking fluids?' Satisfied with Ren's answer, he said, 'I'll have a look, then I'm turning in. If Found continues to improve, I'm off early tomorrow.'

'Where to?' Ren asked Brocket as the other left them.

'He's going back to Raymond, see if he can hurry up getting you and Found to Greta.'

'He's going to a lot of trouble.'

Brocket was silent, looking into the fire.

'But he hasn't been half so much help as you.'

'He had the antibiotics.'

'They wouldn't have been in time if you hadn't forced the pace and taken short cuts. He told me. And he described that gorge. He said he would've been a goner, but you—'

Brocket interrupted, 'What's that bandage for?'

'I've cut myself. With Lil's knife. She found it in your pack and she was trying . . .' But she did not continue, sensing that Brocket was not listening. 'I'll tell you one day.'

He shook his head. 'You'll be gone.'

Ren felt guilty. 'I couldn't live here for ever, could I? I mean –

how could I? – I haven't been brought up here. And you've got Annie Gimmer.'

Brocket kicked at the edge of the fire, making the flames spurt. 'She's dead.'

Ren could not answer him. She did not know what to say.

'Dead and buried. Hilary and me buried her in the cave.' He sat down and fiddled with one of the stakes ready for burning. 'We couldn't lay her very deep in, because of the rock, but there was mud and pebbles to cover her and that had to suffice. We didn't think anything would get to her, not like once. Years and years ago. They found bones there, you see. Layers of them. Elephants and lions and hippopotamuses, then woolly rhinos that came with the ice. There was always some animal or other living in that cave; people, too. Anyway, Mrs Gimmer's there now.'

'Why do you call her Mrs Gimmer, Brocket?'

'That was her name.'

'But she looked after you, as if you were her son.'

'Well, I couldn't call her "mother"; I had to keep that in case the real one turned up.'

'Oh, Brocket.' She put her hands over her face.

'It's not for you to cry about.' He took the stake and poked it among the glowing embers. At last he said, 'And Mrs Gimmer had to go some time. She was very old.'

The tears were washing down Ren's cheeks, dripping off her chin. 'It's not only her, Annie Gimmer.' She was thinking of her own mother, of the new baby, of Found on a dark fell, strapped into the buggy, alone.

'I wish you'd stop it, Ren. You'll start me off.'

She managed, 'I'm sorry. I should be glad. I mean, it's over so I shouldn't be like this. I'll be safe with Greta – '

'Like you wanted, and I'm glad, too.'

' – but you'll be up there, on those fells, by yourself.'

'I shan't. I'll be with Hilary. We've got it all arranged.'

'How?'

'It was his idea. He said, as we are both . . .' Brocket paused to steady his breath, 'as we're both without anyone, we might as well join up. He says I can help him. It's about that book his dad started. Only Hilary has been thinking we could add other things. Not have it just full of the landscape things, other things as well. He says I can say what Mrs Gimmer used to tell me, and that can go in.'

'I'll read it.' Her tears were drying now.

'I'll have to polish up this reading job myself. I'm a bit out of practice.' He added, with some of his former glint, 'It's a day or two since I read a tin. But I'm reminded of something.' He opened his anorak and delved into the lining. 'I pinched this from that library. It's for you.'

In the firelight the cover was warm, rosy; the gilt on the leather spine glinted. Ren turned the pages carefully; they were creamy and soft. 'I can't look at it properly till I've washed my hands.'

'I had a glance at it, but I couldn't make it all out. I expect you can give me the gist.'

'Of course I will.'

'There are pictures, too.'

'Yes.'

Her finger had found the illustration he had stopped at. 'I thought you'd like that one. She looks like you.'

'I'm not so pretty.' She would have liked to say: But you're nicer than this boy is, Brocket; only perhaps he had not thought that he might resemble the boy in the picture, walking with the girl through the wood. 'It's a beautiful book, much better than audio print-outs. I shall read it a lot. I'll read it to Found, too.' He had given her blackberries and a witch stone and now a book. Each time it had been the best possible present. 'I wish I'd something for you.'

He shrugged. 'I don't mind.'

There were movements behind them, then Hilary's voice. 'Lil's having bad dreams. Something to do with a narrow space and since a horse box is no cure for claustrophobia, I've brought her out.'

'I wish you'd leave me alone,' she objected.

'You stopped me getting to sleep.'

'I've never met anyone so bossy.' However, she squatted down by the fire. 'He's even brought blankets,' she mocked as Hilary draped one over her and handed round the rest.

'A fire doesn't keep your back warm,' he said.

'As if I don't know that! I've sat by more fires like this than you've had hot dinners.'

'That wouldn't be difficult, measured by this week,' he told her and they all smiled. 'I'll bring back more food when I've seen Raymond.'

'He's told me,' Lil addressed Ren. 'So Madge hadn't forgotten about you. And that man Raymond says he'll find a home for Found.'

'He thinks Greta might have her as well as me.'

'Yes. That'd be nice.'

'Wouldn't you stay with us too, Lil?'

She shook her head. 'Street people aren't welcome as lodgers.'

'Of course they are,' Hilary protested. 'Where Ren's going, people don't make distinctions.'

She smiled. 'That'd take some getting used to! I don't think I want to give it a try at the moment.'

Brocket asked, 'So what'll you do, Lil?'

'I'm going further north. Where my great-great-grandfather came from. I want to see what it's like. There are lakes; I'll teach myself to swim. So first I'll find the depot where the freight stops for checking and I'll persuade a driver to take me over the border.'

'That's very risky,' Hilary reminded her. 'There must be safer ways. I'll ask Raymond. While you wait for something to be arranged you can shelter in my store. It's more convenient than here for making contacts.'

'You don't have to bother.'

Exasperated, Hilary demanded, 'Why can't you accept a bit of help?'

'I was taught to look after myself.'

'So what?' he snorted. 'It's a pity you didn't learn to take up genuine offers. You should stop being so obstinate.'

'And you should lay off the organising, Hilary.'

'You'd try the patience of a saint.'

'I haven't met one, that I know of, to give it a test.' Then suddenly she laughed. 'But your store sounds better than this horse box, so I'll stay there till we see what this Raymond of yours can fix up.'

'Fine.' Then he blushed. 'I wasn't trying to interfere, you know. Just making suggestions.'

She nodded. For a time they were silent, looking into the fire. 'This is like home was sometimes,' she murmured.

'We ought to go inside,' Brocket said. 'It's growing cold.'

In answer, Lil stretched for more wood and thrust it into the flames.

'You can't stay out all night, Lil.'

'I'm not going in. It's too closed up.'

They recalled her reference to horses chasing her people, herding them in passages from which there was no escape.

'Is that what you were dreaming about?' Ren asked her.

Lil shook her head and kept her eyes on the fire. Its light blanched her cheeks, rawed the bruise on her nose and puckered the scabs, still soft, that laced across her throat. It was possible to imagine that only a few minutes earlier she had returned from her search, bearing Found.

'You ought to have a go at telling us,' Brocket suggested, gentle.

'It can help to . . . sort of break the spell.' He glanced at Hilary. 'It can work.'

'That can't put it right.'

He frowned, trying to understand. 'Put it right?'

Ren whispered, 'Perhaps if you told us, Lil, it wouldn't be so much on your mind.'

'It will always be there. If I tell it, I shall be telling it for Brocket.' She looked at him and considered. 'Annie Gimmer wanted to know how Cob came to be where she is, and I couldn't tell her. Now she is dead, she'll never find out. So perhaps I owe it to Brocket.'

Twenty-four

She crouched by the fire. The others slid nearer. Above them clouds shut away the moon; behind them the darkness billowed impenetrable as black mist; but in their faces was the warm light of the flames. Lil stared at them unblinking. The others watched her, giving her time.

At last she said, 'I've told Ren and Brocket some of it.'

'Hilary knows, too.'

'It was really only the beginning.'

'We guessed.'

'Did I get to the fight?'

'No. Cob was going to put another bandage on her leg.'

Ren said, 'You planned to attack her when she put Found down.'

They remembered her words: 'First I'll jump at her and give a massive clout to the wound; second, while she's rolling in pain and temporarily out of action I'll sink a rabbit punch on her neck; third, grab Found.'

Lil gave a short laugh, mocking herself. 'Plans!'

'Cob guessed them. She dallied over unwinding a length of the hessian from Found and she talked to her. "Who's a bonny baby?" she started off and went on with the usual drivel that some people think babies like till gradually the stuff she was saying changed.

' "I've met some babies in my time. They'd be out on the droveways, striding, hardy and with skin brown as a horse chestnut.

Sometimes I'd join them for a while, sleep under one of the wagons, share their food. They liked my porridge, the little rascals; set them up. You ought to have one of your own, Cob, their people would tell me. But I never had.

'"My grandmother used to say that children are certain cares and uncertain comforts, but that wasn't the reason I didn't have any, flower. I would have borne the cares and rested my hopes on a few comforts. I had to borrow those I had. And they didn't last for ever. There aren't many travellers now walking the moors and fells. I was left with the curlews and a sprinkling of sheep. No children. Till I found Brocket. He wasn't like those striding hardy ones, not when he was left, and he hadn't seen much sun, but he would do, I decided. Properly cared for, he would come on. Then Annie Gimmer turned up and put an end to it."

'I don't know how this makes you three feel, but I tried not to let it sink in. I couldn't afford to feel sorry for her. It was worse, too, because she didn't look so horrible with her head bent over Found.

'She was still going on. "How did she put an end to it? you are asking, flower. Annie pinched him from me, that's what she did. She declared I would tire of him. What a tale! Then she never let him out of her sight till he was grown and fleet. She never gave me a chance to help her bring him up."

'She was sheltering Found from the cold with her great shoulders as she peeled off the cloth, and then zipped her up again and replaced the waterproof covering. Found didn't give a murmur, she handled her so delicate, but I was thinking: This is the same old hag that battered Ren, knocked her out; all her talk about children and Brocket is cunning, trying to soften me up. But I forgot that the moment she held out the strip of hessian and said, lifting the leg, "You bind it, I've no free hand."

'I moved forward. I can't believe now that I could've been such a fool, but I was. I didn't hesitate for a moment to warn myself: This could be another trick. All I thought of was: She says she has no free hand, but I've got two, and now I can get close enough to use them.

'So I stepped across to her. I didn't see the leg swing. It struck me below the knees. Then I was falling, knocked sideways, with the filthy hessian looped round my throat.

'I don't remember much about that fight. It's mostly a jumble of flashes – pictures – while she twisted the noose at the back of my neck. My hands were flailing about but I couldn't aim for her body. Found was still on her lap. That was a handicap for Cob, too. She couldn't get up, use her height against me and overpower me with blows. She had to work from the length of her arm, over Found, at full stretch. So it was good sense to strangle me till I passed out, then tie me up. It seemed hours that I was choking and I reckon you could die from the terror of it as much as from the lack of wind. Your whole body pumps more and more violently but gets nothing; and your head swells and swells till it nearly explodes. All the time her mouth was in my face, open and jagged with tusks. They began to disappear but before I passed out, I got my hands round the noose. I felt points rake down my cheeks, then our hands fought under my chin. There was a squeal from her as a finger snapped. I heard it crack like glass in frost.

'I don't suppose I can have been unconscious more than a few moments. It was her splashing down the stream, so spraying my face with water that woke me up. Therefore I saw where she'd gone. My hands were numb so it took me some time to unfasten her knots and when I'd freed my ankles they refused to hold up my legs. I went the first ten yards along the beck on my knees. I'd seen her pass between high planks of rock; they formed a doorway and leant askew as if they'd fallen from the roof. I crawled into a cavern that was dark as a tomb. I couldn't see Cob but there was something ahead that had delayed her. The light from her lantern reflected on it and cast a weak glint on the wet roof. I felt my way towards it, not noticing that I was wading until I heard the thud of water. I saw that the light was below me and that I was standing on the edge of a tumbling force.'

'Did you climb down?' Brocket asked, awed.

'I half slid, half jumped.'

'I guessed that was where you'd been, but I hoped I was wrong. You could've reached the end of the cave by running along the top.'

'I wasn't to know that. Anyway, I was chasing that woman.'

'Without a light.' He shuddered.

'Flashes came from her lantern when I reached a bend or squeezed past a column. Brocket calls it a cave,' Lil addressed the others, 'but it's nothing like any cave I've heard described. It's a passage, narrow as any alleyway, and arctic, with a draught that pits your skin. As if you're running against hail. Except you don't run. You knock against the sides which have shelves jutting out like blades, and you stumble and trip because the floor is never even; it's never flat; the stream that flows along it hasn't worn a smooth bed. How many thousands of years does it take to do that? Most of the time there isn't a bottom wide enough to take a boot. It's just a fissure, and your boots bridge that, or slide into it and get wedged and you're thrown on your face, struggling to pull the boot out. I didn't see this; it's what I deduced when I fell. And I didn't know how deep the water was. I didn't know whether the cleft would suddenly widen and I'd drop into a deep pit and never be able to climb out.'

'You wouldn't sink much above your knees,' Brocket told her.

'I kept my hands on the sides where I could, but sometimes they touched nothing. I'd found a cavity that wasn't the passage, because when I tried to go down it, I banged my head. When there wasn't a corner between me and her light, I had an idea of what lay in front of me but I couldn't keep up for long: she was moving so fast, 'spite of carrying a baby and a lantern and having a broken finger and a wound in a leg. She must have known every inch of that cave.

'When I did reach stretches without bends, the sight of her was nearly as bad as the darkness and slimy rock. Her breath spouted like smoke in the light of the lantern and she filled the whole passage, an enormous beetle, her coat fanning out like wings, her legs straddling the stream and her boots clinging to the ledges as if fitted with suckers. A bandage would flutter loose and flick behind her. It made me think of a tail or a rope ready to whip.

'Even so, I was desperate to keep close. It wasn't only that I needed the help of her light, I wanted to know that someone else was there. Cob was wild and murderous but I preferred her to the shouts and crashing behind me that I couldn't push out of my head. From the moment I'd dropped down that waterfall and was in that passage, they'd been there. Call them just memories if you like, but they're as bad as what started them. Once you've been forced into some channel – a subway, a drain – and the only way out is blocked, you're stamped with it for always. In any place like it, the sweat, and the smothering in your throat, and the whimpers from your mouth are just the same. And I'm telling you, the shouts and the whistles and the sirens and the hooves ramming me forward and into a funnel echoed as loudly down that cave-passage as the rattles and grunts that Cob made.'

A stake in the fire crackled. They moved closer together.

Brocket and Hilary were thinking: This is as bad as vertigo or Barguest. While Ren remembered how, as they had walked down the railway tunnel, Lil had complained that Annie Gimmer's lantern was feeble and she had been in a frantic hurry to reach the end. She reproached her with: 'I wish you'd told me when we went into the railway tunnel.'

Lil shrugged. 'No point in spreading the fright.'

'A shepherd took me through that cave once,' Brocket said. 'He reckoned it was only about two hundred yards long. It seemed like miles.'

'It did that night. Until I saw a square of the night sky. Outside there was a gap and another passage but she hadn't gone into that. I could see her against the moon, limping, and although there was a good distance between us, I could hear a noise like a thin piping wail. I knew it didn't come from the baby; she never made a sound. This one was squeezed out as if from bellows that are punctured and it would be stopped for a moment by a hiccough of pain. It seemed the most despairing cry I'd ever heard.

'But I was wrong.'

Lil bowed her head and drew the blanket over her neck. Her hands trembled.

Ren leant to her. 'You don't have to tell us, Lil. I'll stay out here with you while you sleep.'

Lil shook her head. 'Cob was moving very slowly but I couldn't gain on her. I was drenched to the bone and freezing; I had to force my feet for every step. By that time I couldn't think. I just functioned. Hoping the muscles wouldn't give up. I wasn't able to work out tactics, plans, anything of that kind. I didn't wonder what might happen next. I dragged forward mechanically. After all, this couldn't continue for ever. One of us would drop down soon and I didn't much care which.

'We had crossed over curving ground and were running by the side of a beck. It went along a shallow course several feet wide and towards trees I could see on the skyline. Very soon we had almost reached them; they formed a small copse at the crest of a knoll. The beck flowed towards it and we had almost gained the spot where it seemed to disappear at the base of the knoll when I stumbled and sent pebbles clattering.

'She swung round and shouted, "I thought I'd seen the last of you.

Get off my heels, will you! I've given you a taste of what to expect."

'I didn't answer. We both stopped.

' "I should've polished you off. Get away with you!" She was screaming, mad with frustration. "This baby's mine. I had her first."

'I said, "Not for long. You parked her. By the peat road."

'She was yelling curses but I didn't listen. I was remembering how she had hunted us down and how Ren had missed Madge through leaving the cave, and how this old hag's cunning had fetched me away from the barn so that only Ren was left, and how we had looked after Found.

'Then I heard her say, "You'll rue your interference this night," and I watched her place the lantern on the grass and spread out the waterproof and lay Found upon it and tuck the cloths round her. Then she backed a few steps from her and faced me upstream.

' "You want her. I do. She goes to the one that wins," she announced and put up her fists.

'I don't know whether any of you've done any boxing.'

'I have, a little,' Hilary murmured.

They looked at him, astonished. Lil said, 'Well, it isn't something we are taught: fists aren't much good against dogs or whips or truncheons. Or against bullets. But I'd watched a bit of casual sparring and that had to suffice. When I finally stood in front of her I raised my arm as a guard and managed to ward off the first punch. Then she came in, had her arms round me and was pounding away at my back. I couldn't unlatch myself and I realised that she intended to throw me to the ground and somehow finish me off. She swung me round so that her shadow didn't fall on my face and she found enough breath to crow: "You're bloody! My nails can tatter flesh."

'Then I was kicked off my feet and bent like a sapling over a platform of stone.'

'Oh, Lil,' Ren moaned.

Lil stared at her and frowned, then put a hand over her eyes. 'I'm sorry, Ren. It's not your face I see.

'Hers was above me, still topped by that greasy cap and so close that it blocked out the moon. I could make out the tufts of hairs in the nostrils and the skin in ridges down the cheeks and the teeth that were broken and brown as rust. Through them, her breath whistled and sickened me with its stench. No matter how hard I pushed with my hands, I couldn't shift her. I hadn't enough space to swing at her; all I could do was beat my fists on her shoulders and upper arms. She didn't flinch. I was like a mouse flattened by a cat's paw, then released for a second to wriggle before being cuffed back into place. Her fingers climbed up my chest; I could see the broken one dragging, then they fastened on my throat.

'She hissed, "I've a mind to do you in this time, but I wouldn't rest easy. I've roved the dales all my life and I'll not take to the manner of the pack you run with." Her hands dropped. She grabbed one of my wrists and with a great heave pushed me half-round, forced the arm behind me and up my back.

'I heard myself screaming but I could hear something else. It was the voice of the man who had trained us. It told me not to tense against the pain but go with it, act as if I was finished, and then there was a chance the opponent would relax. So I let my shoulders go.

'She was saying: "I don't wish for blood on my conscience when I'm tending the child. So it's a case of seeing you can't hinder," but I was listening to my instructor's voice. It was reminding me that this was not a competition to prove who was better, winning or losing; it was about who got up at the end and who could not. And the sole of my boot found a ledge of stone; it gave me a purchase and, still under her, I pushed against it. In this way I forced my hips and bum backwards a little. Her weight was still on me; she was still pushing my arm; the pain was still lancing through it, but I realised that if I went on pushing back, the tension of her hold on me would

212

be reduced. And I was right. Before she could change her position I'd managed to slide from under her, unwinding myself from her grip. As I did so, I brought up a knee and punched at her with my boot. It hit her in the belly, doubled her up and knocked her back. Then she was in the stream, winded, thrashing about, the wounded leg stiff and clumsy; it twisted and jerked.

'I scrambled towards her knowing that somehow I had to follow up this advantage. I could see the blood spurting out of the wound and into the water, which swirled past her, frothed behind her then suddenly disappeared. And I saw why it disappeared. It was pouring over an edge. But she was trying to get upright again, only the leg wouldn't bear her. She tottered, skidded among pebbles, crashed down. Her hands dived into the beck, the fingers scrabbled for a hold on the slippery stone, but she was already sliding. It was completely quiet. I watched her, amazed, and she stared back at me as she went into the water. It seemed a long time before there was silence again after that long, splitting shriek.'

No one spoke. They wished they could shut out the scene she had described.

'I dared not get closer to where she had fallen. All I could see was the beck folding over, then it was gone. I walked a little way from it and climbed up the knoll. From there I had a view. By then I knew what to expect, but my imagination could never have prepared me for what I saw. Brocket knows.'

Hilary turned to him. 'A pothole?' His voice hardly lifted above the put-put of the flames.

'Yes. It's a vertical shaft. Mrs Gimmer said it's three hundred feet down. There's a pool at the bottom, fed by a fall you can't see, as well as the one from that top gill.'

'She didn't have a chance.'

'It's perhaps as well,' Brocket said grimly. 'There's no way out.'

'If I hadn't kicked her, she wouldn't have fallen into the beck.

She wouldn't have slipped. She had said she didn't intend to do me in. She spared me. She was just putting me out of action, but I was remembering instructions. So I kicked out. Don't you see? If I hadn't done that, she wouldn't be dead.' Her voice was shrill; it jangled their heads with echoes of that last hopeless shriek.

Eventually Brocket managed: 'You weren't to know that would happen, Lil. From a kick.'

'She wouldn't have toppled over if I hadn't given her the wound,' Ren whispered.

After a time, calmer, Lil added, 'Annie Gimmer had it worked out. She'd found the lantern. She'd seen the cap; it must've caught on a ledge or shrub as Cob went down. Therefore she knew where Cob was and she seemed to give up. Because Cob was dead. I didn't like her, but she'd been good, looking after Brocket.'

'She was ready to give up,' Hilary suggested. 'She knew Brocket could fend for himself.'

'I bet she wished I'd never come. So do I.'

'Well, I'm glad you did,' Ren said.

'I couldn't stand it any longer on the streets. I was trying to get away, but there was the baby and I got dragged in. Then look what happened.'

'It hasn't been all loss,' Hilary murmured. 'There have been benefits.'

As he spoke, a sound came from the horse box. At first it was no more than a rustle of breath, a sigh which sharpened into a cough to clear the throat. Ren got up. 'Found's awake.'

The noise was growing into a grumble; it swelled as the lungs filled. 'She's winding herself up for yell,' Brocket said.

'It means she's getting better.' Ren discovered that her weariness had vanished and her body was no longer stiff and cold but supple and warm. Stretching her arms, she sieved the darkness through her fingers. It was silken, feathery, soft as gauze.

Then Found's cry became a wail, hungry, demanding, amplified by the wooden panels of the horse box and thrilling their ears.

'Listen to that!' Brocket admired. 'She could get prizes for it.'

'I think we should have the prizes,' Hilary said.

'Except there aren't many going in these parts.' Lil mimicked Brocket's voice.

And suddenly they were laughing although their cheeks were covered with tears, and the blankets had fallen away from their shoulders, and they were jumping, beating their feet into the grass, clapping their hands, leaping together like children careless round the sparks of a bonfire, under a guardian sky.

Waterbound

Jane Stemp

The City is a place of rules, a place where Admin is always watching . . . a place where there is no room to be different.

Under the City, the river flows from light into dark, into an unknown place. A place which hides a secret. Something forbidden – out of sight and out of mind.

There Gem finds the Waterbound, the children the City forgot. She joins in their fight to be part of the world she knows.

Why are they underground? Is there a way out?